EDITED AND COVER BY ...

To contact Michael, please email:
subscribers@michaelrobertson.co.uk

Edited by:

Pauline Nolet - http://www.paulinenolet.com

Cover design by Dusty Crosley - https://www.deviantart.com/dustycrosley

COPYRIGHT

Between Fury and Fear: Book eight of Beyond These Walls

Michael Robertson
© Michael Robertson 2020

Between Fury and Fear: Book eight of Beyond These Walls is a work of fiction. The characters, incidents, situations, and all dialogue are entirely a product of the author's imagination, or are used fictitiously and are not in any way representative of real people, places, or things.

Any resemblance to persons living or dead is entirely coincidental.

All rights reserved.

No part of this publication may be reproduced, stored in a retrieval system, or transmitted in any form or by any means electronic, mechanical, photocopying, recording, or

BETWEEN FURY AND FEAR: BOOK EIGHT OF BEYOND THESE WALLS

A POST-APOCALYPTIC SURVIVAL THRILLER

MICHAEL ROBERTSON

otherwise, without the prior written permission of the author except in the case of brief quotations embodied in critical articles and reviews.

CHAPTER 1

William's shoulder ached, but he had this. Olga, Max, Gracie, and Artan were behind him. They might have meant to give their support, but they stood in a semicircle of scrutiny, judging his every step as he tiptoed through the long grass. He held his breath, his heart beating in his throat. One step at a time, he edged forwards. The blood drained from his right arm, and it tingled with the threat of pins and needles. But he continued to hold the spear aloft in his tight grip. His too tight grip. The memory of Artan's teaching rang through his mind. *Relax! Be at one with the weapon.*

Too much closer and he'd spook the fox. He had to rely on his aim. William's legs shook as he took his next step, touching down with just the tip of his right toe. He held his balance. Three … Two … He threw the spear. Hard. *Thwip!*

William's entire frame sank as he put his heel down. His shot missed the creature by several feet. "Sh—"

But his words were cut off by Olga's spear. Launched from at least ten feet farther back, it sailed past him. The tip slammed into the side of the fox's head, went straight through its skull, and pinned it to the soft ground.

Hawk clapped, and Artan slapped Olga on the back as he said, "Good shot."

William returned to the only job he could do while they were out in the wild lands. He gathered up the legs of the deer Gracie had killed earlier, and he dragged it along with them.

Artan and Hawk jogged over. They each took one end of the creature.

William kept his focus on the ground while saying, "I'm fine." But he let them lift the deer and lay it along the back of his shoulders.

Hawk walked off while Artan rested a hand on William's back. "You want me to help you?"

William shook his head. He shivered from where the day had grown long, the wind picking up in the open meadow. "I need to do this. At least it'll keep me warm, eh?"

The weight of the deer now too much, William stared at Jezebel on the ground. Artan grabbed his weapon too and put it in his right hand. He slapped William's back. "At least it's not a stag."

William rolled his eyes. "Imagine!"

A deep orange glow seared the evening sky, the setting sun obscured by the tall buildings in the ruined city. They'd spent the past few weeks on its periphery, growing stronger through rest and food.

"I think we've done enough hunting for the day," Gracie said.

Every time she spoke, Olga's face twisted like a mocking child. If Gracie noticed, and if she cared, she hid it well. Her voice chipper, she added, "We really don't want to be out here when it gets dark."

They'd been following Gracie's lead for the past few

weeks since they'd left Grandfather Jacks' palace. Even when they'd stopped to let Matilda rest up so she could heal, Gracie had taken charge. Most of them were comfortable with it. She'd shown them where to hunt, and they'd eaten well. They had food, they had water from a nearby lake, and they had each other. It had been a simple existence and exactly what they'd needed. But the fact remained; they had to move on sooner rather than later.

Gracie took the lead with Artan at her side. They were heading back towards their ruined city. Olga and Hawk were next in line, and William took up the rear, sweating beneath the weight of the deer's carcass.

While derelict, the city was far more modern than the ruins on the outskirts of Edin. Many of the towers were taller than any buildings William had seen north of the funnel. Some of them stood hundreds of feet tall. Skeletons of what they once were, but they maintained their structural integrity. At night-time, when the wind picked up, the place wailed a haunting symphony. Some nights it kept him awake. He grunted with the effort of carrying the deer. At least he could guarantee one thing: tonight he'd sleep like the dead.

William focused on the ground a few feet ahead of him and fell from one step into the next. The deer pressed down on his shoulders. Aches stabbed the base of his skull, and his head spun. He paused. As had the others.

It came again. A moan of discontent. A tired and sad groan. A small cluster of trees stood on their left. The shadows in the fading light were deep enough to hide the creature.

Artan, Olga, and Gracie raised their spears. William gripped Jezebel tighter.

Hawk took off, charging away from the group.

Gracie launched her spear. It shot past the attacking hunter and stuck into the diseased. It remained horizontal for a second before the creature fell onto its back, the spear now pointing straight up at the sky.

"What the hell was that?" Olga said.

"I hit it, didn't I?"

"And you nearly hit Max."

"Careful, love," Gracie said, her eyebrows raised. "Call him that in front of Max and there will be trouble."

"Obviously I meant Hawk." Olga tutted. Her face turned red as she spat her retort. "Hawk!"

And maybe the argument would have continued like many had over the past few weeks, but Hawk's yell pulled them away from one another.

"Hawk?" Olga said. "What the hell are you playing at?"

Feet from the cluster of trees, Hawk pulled his knife from his belt, dropped his spear, and tackled another diseased to the ground. The shadows had hidden it from William's sight. Hawk repeatedly stabbed the creature in the head, each attack sinking into it with a deep squelch.

Thwip! Artan loosed his spear. It flew true, again showing William the location of yet another diseased. Like the one Gracie had nailed, Artan's diseased fell backwards, the spear pointing straight up.

Hawk painted a stocky silhouette. His broad shoulders rose and fell with his ragged breaths. He held his thick fists at his sides as he strolled back to the others. His lust for violence remained balled in his tight frame.

"What the fuck was that all about?" Olga said. "*Again!*"

"I wanted—" Hawk caught his breath "—to make sure the diseased didn't reach us."

"That's what your spear's for. You know that better than most. Who are you trying to impress by wrestling it to the ground? You make it much harder for any of us to fight it. Gracie nearly killed you."

Gracie shook her head. "No I didn't."

Since they'd left the asylum, Hawk had developed a blind determination to help his friends. He'd thrown himself into danger at even the slightest hint of trouble. He could protect them, so he would. He'd screwed up in Umbriel when he'd turned on them, yet they still helped him free Dianna. He owed them all. At least, that was how he saw it. He shrugged. "I'm okay."

Her face red, her eyes wide, and even in the poor light William traced the spittle spraying from Olga's mouth when she pointed back the way Hawk had come from. "Did you even see that one Artan took down?"

"Yeah." The light might have saved his lie had Hawk not spun around to watch Artan retrieve his spear.

Artan returned with his and Gracie's weapons. The pair of them wiped the tips clean in the long grass while Hawk and Olga glared at one another.

"Come on," Gracie said, "let's go."

∽

THEIR PAUSE for Hawk to demonstrate his fighting skills had given William a much-needed rest. But now they'd set off again, he sweated as much as before. The darkness closed in, turning their city into a silhouette. The three most prominent buildings were a line of tall towers, the landmark William had used to orientate himself these past few weeks. He looked at them today from a new angle. It took several deep breaths to find his words. "Where are we going?"

Gracie had begun an ascent up a short hill. "I'll show you in a minute."

"You hadn't planned on telling us you were taking a different route?" Olga said. "I thought you said we were heading back to the city?"

Dew coated the long grass, turning William's trousers

damp. The weight of the deer on his back pushed every step into the soft ground.

"Will you just shut up for a minute?" Gracie said.

"What did you say?" Olga halted her climb directly in front of William. He stumbled to the side and went around her. Break his momentum now and he wouldn't start again.

Gracie reached the crest, Artan and Hawk stopping on either side of her.

His lungs already tight, William lost more air at what he saw.

As Olga joined them, Gracie said, "I wanted to bring you here in poor light so you can see what we're dealing with."

A large city sat in the distance, on the edge of the ruins they'd been staying in. A tall wall surrounded it. Dark grey, thick, and impenetrable, it had been made from the same steel as the funnel. Light burst from within its walls, shining up into the sky like the head of a giant torch. This city stretched wider than the ruins it bordered.

The wind was stronger for them being at the top of the small hill. It turned William's sweat cold against his skin, his eyelids tacky with each blink. "How the hell are we supposed to get around that?"

"And what the hell is it?" Olga said.

A check from one side to the other, Gracie threw one more glance at the vast city in the distance and said, "We shouldn't be talking about this here. They might see us."

"From all the way over there?" Olga said.

"There are many things you don't know about what lies ahead."

"Well, instead of holding onto all the secrets like the smug bitch you are, how about you share some of those things?"

"First, I want to only say it once, so let me say it to everyone at the same time. Second, there are a lot of things for you to adjust to ahead. If I went into detail explaining all of those, we'd be here for another three months. If you come with me, you can see it for yourself when we travel farther south. Le—"

Gracie got cut off by a loud *boom!* An orange glow from an explosion near the three towers in the city. Grey smoke lifted into the sky.

"What the hell was that?" Hawk said.

"Let's get back to the others, and I'll tell you everything in as much detail as I can."

Olga opened her mouth to reply, but Gracie had already jogged away down the hill. Hawk followed her.

William stepped in their direction.

"Come on," Artan said to Olga, pulling on their fiery friend's arm. "Let's at least get out of their line of sight."

Gracie and Hawk a little way ahead of them, Olga said, "Are we sure we trust Gracie on this one?"

"Not sure, no," Artan said.

"But what else do we have?" William added. "She's led us true so far."

"Like they did in Umbriel?"

"We can't assume everyone's going to screw us over like they did in Umbriel," Artan said. "Here." He stood close to William to allow him to slide the deer across to him. Moving off as if the heavy carcass weighed nothing, the boy, two years William's junior and a skinny as a spear, ran down the hill after Hawk and Gracie.

"Come on," William said, pulling Olga along with him before he gripped Jezebel with both hands. He might not have the skills to throw a spear, but he could still remove heads with his axe. "Let's get back to the others."

CHAPTER 2

The sun had finally set, and William sat next to Matilda as part of a larger semicircle around the fire in the wrecked house. Half of its roof had fallen in. Despite the buildings inside the city having fared better against entropy, Gracie had insisted they stay there. It kept them from entering the ruins before they were ready, and because it had a fireplace on the first floor, it kept them away from the diseased and allowed them to cook what they caught at the end of each day.

The deer William and Artan had carried hissed and spat over the flames. Outside, the cool breeze played the still city, whistling through the empty windows and rattling anything that hung loose. It toyed with the flames in the fireplace, turning their hypnotic sway erratic. A strong gust shot down the chimney. It squashed the flames, the fire vomiting a shower of sparks out onto the floor in front of them.

They'd been there long enough to build the fire, light it, and prepare the deer. Gracie had had plenty of time, but she hadn't yet told the others about the vast community on the outskirts of the ruined city. She'd not mentioned the explosion. "Can people see the flames?" William said.

"Like who?" Max asked.

Gracie's eyes narrowed slightly before she shook her head. "No. Because this building is on the outskirts of the city and opens up onto the plains, you can only see us from the north. And the night hides the smoke coming from the chimney."

The silence swelled with anticipation, Gracie's cue to continue. William looked from Artan, to Olga, and then to Hawk. Each of them fixed on Gracie, but she stared at the flames.

Max had the ointment they'd taken from Grandfather Jacks' palace. He dabbed it on his burns on his left pec and thigh before handing it to Matilda. "You finish it."

Red-faced, Hawk clenched his jaw and stared at the ground as the two passed the jar between them. He'd been too familiar with that ointment as a child, the slashes around his neck evidence of Grandfather Jacks' brutal regime.

No need for a bandage now, Matilda upended the jar, tipping the rest of the ointment on what remained of the cut on her thigh. Both her and Max were almost fully healed, and they could have moved off a few days ago, but better to be sure. The flames cast deep shadows across her tense face, but she didn't wince like she had when treating her wound previously. "Does it feel better?" William said.

Although Matilda smiled before she replied, Hawk took the empty pot from beside her and launched it into the city through the hole in the roof with a, "Yeargh!"

The group held their breath, the wind and the crackle from the fire the only sound until a gentle *splash* reported the pot's landing.

"I've lived in my community my entire life," Gracie said. "My dad runs the place."

"What's it called?" Matilda said.

"Dout."

Olga muttered from the side of her mouth, "That's encouraging."

"It's an underground community," Gracie continued. "We can't compete with the larger settlements around us, so we live an undercover existence."

"Like snakes in the grass?" Olga said.

Gracie continued, "But anyway, you'll all get to see it soon." She leaned forwards, "So tell me, how did you all meet?"

William turned his palms to the sky. What about the settlement they saw earlier? What did she have to tell them about the ruined city they were about to go through? He opened his mouth to challenge her, but Matilda cut him off.

"William and I met at school when we were tiny."

It took him back. Back to their first classroom. Back to their childhood when he dreamed of being a protector. When he looked forward to national service. He smiled. "And I noticed you from the very second I saw you."

Matilda blushed. "No you didn't. You called me names and pulled my hair."

Clearing his throat and straightening a pretend tie, William said, "Those were my finest moves. You should consider yourself lucky to have experienced them."

"Is that what you call it?" Matilda said.

"Well, I'm sorry." William cleared his throat and dropped his gaze. "But what I wanted to say is if love at first sight is a thing, it hit me with both barrels the day I met you."

"You were five," Matilda said.

William shrugged. "It took me a while to work it out."

Olga made retching noises and Matilda blushed.

"I met Max, William, and Matilda during national service in Edin," Olga said.

"National service?" Gracie tilted her head to one side. "What's that?"

Olga snorted an ironic laugh. "Something that seemed far more important than it was. None of that bullshit mattered after Edin fell."

"How did Edin fall?" Gracie said.

"Hugh," Olga said. When only the wind answered her, she added, "William and Matilda had left Edin because they thought they had nothing left. Hugh found out Artan was still—"

"We don't need to tell that story," Matilda said.

"No." Artan leaned forwards, the light from the fire highlighting his brow and casting a shadow across his eyes. "We do."

Matilda sighed and leaned back.

"Can I?" Olga said.

"Bit late to be asking," Matilda said.

Olga drew a deep breath in through her nose. "When Hugh found out you were still alive, he left Edin to find William and Matilda. They thought you were dead; otherwise they never would have left."

"And he left the gate open?" Artan said.

Olga nodded. "You guessed it."

"*Shit!*"

"We were going to tell you, Artan," Matilda said.

"That Edin fell because of me?"

"Because of *Hugh*. He was stupid, and he left the gate to the national service area open. *He* let the diseased in, not you."

"But he wouldn't have done it were it not for me."

"That was his choice," Matilda said. "You had no control over that."

As much as William wanted to say something to diffuse

the situation, he had no words. Max came to the rescue when he said, "My entire family turned."

Artan had been leaning into the semicircle, glaring at Matilda. He pulled back into the shadows.

"I had to end them all," Max went on, telling the floor rather than those around him. Those who'd been with him in Edin knew the story, but Dianna, Hawk, and Gracie watched on, Gracie with her mouth hanging wide. "I had to kill every one of them, and now, when I'm surrounded by diseased, I always see their faces."

Cyrus had already told them as much, which Max didn't know. Olga, who sat beside the traumatised boy, reached over to put her arm around him. But he shifted away. Since Cyrus' death and his time in the Asylum, he'd withdrawn from everyone.

William jumped when Dianna cleared her throat. Her voice soft, she said, "I grew up in Umbriel. Rita and Mary raised me."

The slightest smile cut across Hawk's strong features at the mention of the two women.

"They were the best two mums I could have ever wished for."

Hawk laughed. "I felt like they were mums for the entire community. The hunters might have provided the food, but that place would have gone to shit were it not for them." His smile fell. "I wonder what they're doing now."

"Probably the same as always." Dianna laughed this time. "They're probably keeping that place running. Keeping everyone in check."

Gracie reached across and laid her hand over the back of Dianna's. "Who are your real mum and dad?"

Dianna shook her head. "I don't know. Rita and Mary. But as far as biological parents go, I'm guessing Grandfather Jacks is my father."

"But he wanted to …" William said.

Hawk raised an eyebrow. "You sound surprised." His delivery turned several degrees colder as he transitioned from question to accusation. "After all we saw."

William went back to seeing the boys in the cage. The flames in front of him blurred with his loss of focus. He spoke in a voice he recognised as his own, even if he didn't connect to the delivery. "Yeah, I suppose." They'd gone on too long. The world returned to a sharper focus. He lifted one side of his bottom and pulled the map in the plastic sleeve from his back pocket. He spread it out on the floor in front of them. "Gracie, where is your community on here?"

"I can't show you. It's a secret."

"Well, that's a recommendation to go if ever I've heard one," Olga said.

"But if you come with me, I can show you. Everyone in Dout has sworn to keep the place secret. It's the only way we've survived as long as we have. We live in the shadows of larger cities, and we move in the darkness. What were your plans when you came through the funnel?"

"We were heading south," William said, drawing a line with his finger across the map, tracing where the wall bisected the land.

"Anything more specific than that?"

"South of the wall."

Gracie laughed. But when no one else joined in, her face fell. "You're being serious, aren't you?"

"Of course."

"Okay, well, one step at a time."

"We've waited long enough," William said. "So how about we take that first step? How about you tell us what that city on the edge of these ruins is all about?"

"I wanted to make sure you'd had one last rest before I told you about them."

"We've rested. We're ready to hear it."

While Matilda, Max, and Dianna watched on, the others nodded their agreement with William.

Gracie straightened her back and filled her lungs, her chest rising with her inhale. "Okay. I suppose there's never going to be a good time."

CHAPTER 3

William sat with the others, waiting for Gracie to speak. She stood up, the crackle and hiss of the fire highlighting her silence. The flames rippled in the wind. She walked to a large window looking out across the city. It must have had glass in it at some point, but no traces of it remained.

William followed her over, and one by one, the others joined. Matilda came to William's side, slipping her hand into his.

Almost every building in this place stood taller than any William had seen. Many of them challenged his beliefs of what he'd thought possible. "It's a wonder none of them fall down."

When Gracie turned to William, he said, "In Edin, a structure any taller than a few stories would collapse. We built a few larger structures, but lots of families died beneath the weight of falling rubble when the design of their homes grew too ambitious."

"Steel helps," Gracie said.

The empty window funnelled the wind. William clamped his jaw against its chill and shivered. "I can see."

"So, this is the last part of the journey," Gracie said. "One of the shortest parts too."

Olga turned her palms to the sky, her face twisting as she spat her question. "But?"

Thankfully, Gracie didn't bite. "*But* it's probably the trickiest part."

Matilda leaned closer to the ginger girl. "Trickier than dealing with a horde of diseased with an injured leg?"

Dianna had turned pale. "Trickier than getting out of the asylum?"

Gracie's silence offered little comfort.

Any trace of daylight had died on the horizon, the silhouettes of buildings dominating the old city's skyline. Sentries from a bygone era. They now served as a memory of what had once been. But they held much more. They had a new role in this new world. They were shelter from the hard wind, and they created shadows for an enemy's ambush attack.

"I know I keep focusing on the buildings," William said, "but *why* are they so tall?"

"This is how people used to live. Why build out when you can build up? It's a much more efficient use of space, and in a time when cities were expanding, it made sense. Even now, with all the walled communities, growing a city's footprint is a logistical nightmare."

National service flooded William's mind. A glance at Matilda, he said, "Tell us about it."

William only realised his jaw hung open when Matilda urged it closed with a gentle press against the bottom of his chin. "You okay?" she said.

"I was just imagining…"

The others all turned his way.

"I mean, we saw what the diseased did to Edin. Imagine what it did to this place? Imagine being trapped in one of those towers with the diseased coming in on the ground floor."

Max stared through the window like the rest of them. Tears stood in his glazed eyes.

"What were those three enormous towers used for, Gracie?" William said.

"People used to work in them."

"Huh?" The faces of those around William mirrored his shock. "What useful work can you do in a place like that?"

A slight smile played with the left side of Gracie's mouth. "Now that's a question I'm not sure I can answer. When this city was thriving, people used to pack themselves into trains and cars and busses—"

"What are they?" Olga said.

"Modes of transport." Gracie shrugged. "Vehicles that moved people around the city. So the people would travel en masse to their places of work. Buildings like those three towers. They'd sit down all day, talking to people, and making money from things that didn't exist. They earned a living off industries like insurance."

Max's focus returned. "What's insurance?"

"If someone hurts themselves, they get money. And if they hurt someone else, the other person gets money."

"So, many people earned a living by hurting themselves?"

Gracie smiled and shook her head. "It doesn't matter. It was pointless then, and it's even more pointless now. Times were different. Those in power were overweight, had health conditions, and wore suits. Their weapons of choice were laptops and briefcases."

"Laptops?" Olga said. "Briefcases?"

"Silly little lockable boxes with handles," Gracie said. "Ridiculous and impractical things. Anyway, we're getting off track. We don't have time for a history lesson. My point is, the three tallest towers belonged to an insurance company. They were a big deal at one point."

"Hence the phallic monuments celebrating their status?" Matilda said.

Gracie rolled her eyes. "Exactly."

Artan, whose shoulders had remained slumped from when he'd been told about Hugh leaving the gate open, sighed. "It all seems so redundant now."

"So what about the city on the outskirts?" William said. "The one we saw when out hunting?" He turned to Matilda and Max while pointing away from them. "There's a city over there. Just over the brow of that hill. We can't see it because of the lay of the land. It's surrounded by a thick steel wall like the funnel."

"And it's not the only one," Gracie said.

William spun around so fast he forgot to let go of Matilda's hand and tugged her around with him. "Huh?"

"There's another city of similar size on the other side of the ruins. They call themselves Fear"—she pointed to her left—"and Fury." She pointed right.

"Defensive much?" Olga said. "They should have just called themselves *fuck off* and *leave us alone.*"

Even Max smiled at the comment.

Gracie snorted a laugh, and Olga scowled at her. "We call them Tweedledee and Tweedledum."

Mumbling beneath her breath, Olga said, "I prefer my versions."

"So do I."

"I'm not your friend!" Olga's outburst forced Gracie back a step.

Artan manoeuvred himself between the two. "So what's their story?"

After a lingering glare at Olga, Gracie said, "Everyone

used to live in this city in front of us. But things changed when the diseased came. Capitalism—the way they ran their society—died. Suddenly no one had any use or any skills. They turned on one another. First, it started with fights in the streets. It soon escalated into an all-out war. There were too many people, in too small a space, with too much time on their hands. Their natural division fell along lines of class."

"Class?" Matilda said.

All the while, the city wailed and howled as if nature tried to revive it.

The right side of Gracie's face bulged from where she pushed her tongue into her cheek. "Wealth is probably the easiest way to describe it. Wealth and privilege. The rich went one way and took their armies and politicians with them. The workforce went the other. At first they moved to either side of the city, a divide between them. A strip of no-man's-land. But what neither one knew was the other had been building a safer place to live on the outskirts of town on their side. A walled city into which they could retreat. Apparently they were virtually mirroring one another in how they built their communities."

"Fear and Fury?" William said.

"Right."

"And who remained in the city?"

"No one. The strip of no-man's-land grew wider and wider until that's all the city was. They'd built their defences, they had an empty city between them, and ever since then—"

A loud boom and flash of fire in the distance. They all jumped back. All of them save Gracie.

Olga's eyes widened, and her face turned puce. She pointed out of the window. "What the fuck was that?"

Although Gracie stared out in the explosion's direction, the light died as quickly as it had appeared. "Probably another battle between the two communities. They've both left the city, but the fighting hasn't stopped."

"Are they trying to get control of the place?" Matilda said.

"No." Gracie shook her head. "It works for both of them if neither has control. They're fighting because they're worried if they don't, the other side will perceive them as weak and try to take their city. It's a war without end, and many people lose their lives because of it. Each city sends small groups of fighters out to humiliate and dominate the other in the hope it will scare them into never attempting a full-on war. Those in the army are cannon fodder for the cause. Getting caught by the enemy is the worst way to die."

"So why do people fight in the war?" Matilda said. "Why don't they just say no?"

"Like we said no to national service?" William said.

Olga stepped closer to Gracie and looked her up and down. "And you're confident you can get us through to the other side?"

"We rarely lose people on our way through the ruins, and we pass through here often. This is where we come when we want to stock up on our supplies of meat. I've done this run plenty of times."

"And even you got caught and ended up in Grandfather Jacks' community," Olga said.

"That was the nomads. When we were out hunting, a horde of diseased split our group, and I ran into the nomads. I was a fool to trust them."

"Like we're fools to trust you?" Her balled fists on her hips, Olga stepped so close to Gracie they were nearly touching one another.

Gracie shrugged. "That's for you to decide. I can only tell you what my intention is. You need to choose if you trust that. I want to get home. If you come with me, you will be welcome in my community and can stay for as long as you like. Dad will be grateful for how you've helped me get away from Grandfather Jacks."

Before Olga could speak again, William said, "And if we go with you, when's the best time to do it?"

"We should go now," Gracie said. "Matilda and Max are much better and ready for the journey. And we're safer at night. It's the best time to move through the city."

"Like that explosion just proved!" Olga rolled her eyes and shook her head.

"I've been away from my family for too long now." Gracie turned to face the city again. "Whatever you decide, I'm going back home. If you're coming with me, I need you to listen to me and follow my guidance."

William threw a hard glare at Olga, who closed her mouth and stepped back a pace.

"So make your mind up," Gracie said. "Are you coming or not?"

CHAPTER 4

William stepped through the doorway last, leaving the ruined house behind as he joined the others. For the first time in the two weeks they'd been staying there, they exited towards the towers and blocks rather than with their backs to them. Sure, they'd only gotten a few feet closer, and they'd seen this and more from the first-floor window, but they'd stepped into a new world. Jezebel in one hand, he rested her shaft against his right shoulder to help him bear the weight of her heavy axe head. For what good she'd do in the tight and dark streets …

A tower block to their right remained mostly intact save for the windows. The wind howled through all the open spaces, playing it like a vast ocarina. This old city might have been a graveyard, but it showed William enough. If only he could have seen it in its day. It must have been magnificent.

As their leader, Gracie had the group's attention. They'd agreed they'd follow her … when she finally decided to move off. She currently wrapped a large slab of the remaining deer meat in an old piece of fabric.

"You expect us to eat that?" Olga pointed at it with her sword.

"I expect nothing of you. You're your own person. You've told me as much more times than I care to remember."

"What's that supposed to mean?"

"You have opinions, Olga."

"And I don't mind sharing them!"

"*That's* my point."

"That's a good thing."

"Maybe for someone arrogant enough to think their opinions are always correct."

And who could blame Gracie for getting cross? William's patience would have run out much sooner. Olga had gone at her for weeks now.

Before Olga replied, Gracie said, "This route isn't easy, but it's the best route through the city. Like I said up there"—she pointed back at the first-floor window of the house they'd just left—"I need you all to listen to me and do as I say. If you don't—" she paused and levelled a stare on Olga "—then that's your choice. I have my path through here. You either follow me or you don't. I won't change what I'm doing if people are too pig-headed to listen."

Olga rolled her shoulders, pulled them back, and lifted her chest. She jutted her chin in Gracie's direction, her lips tight as she sniffed.

"We will listen to you," William said.

Everyone but Olga nodded their agreement.

William scrunched his nose when Gracie used some twine to tie the chunk of meat to her back, the slab of cooked deer the size of a rucksack. Would the others eat it with her? Although, easy to turn his nose up on a full stomach. He'd been hungry before. He might be grateful for it later.

A cracked two-lane road separated them from the rest of the city. Gracie looked one way and then the other as if checking for traffic. Her steps were damn near soundless when she crossed.

The first building they came to had a large hole where the window had once been. At least twenty feet wide and ten feet tall, Gracie led them in, William and the others jumping in after her, their weapons ready should they need them.

What had once been tables and chairs now existed as twisted and rusting frames. The old furniture's skeletons. Bolted into the concrete floor, they now clung on in defiance of their battle with entropy. The remains of several booths ran along one side of the room. Each one identical, each one containing a large metal box bolted to the wall. William pointed at them. "What are they?"

"This place used to be a café."

The others leaned around William to better hear Gracie's whispers. He said, "A what?"

"A place where people came for drinks and food. They were utterly pointless. They served drinks no one needed and food that had little nutritional value, but tasted nice. Apparently"—she pointed at the wall of booths—"you'd go into that pod, and those machines had small screens on them. You'd pick what you wanted from the screens, and the machine would spit it out for you. Hard to imagine now, isn't it? Before everything went to shit, everyone had so much to eat and drink, they were more worried about how fat people were getting than feeding them."

Artan turned full circle, his mouth hanging open, his spear at his side. "So people gathered here, like in a meeting hall?"

"Kinda. Although, from what we understand, while many people were in the same place together, they gathered in smaller groups. They were much less communal than we are. Mass gatherings were commonplace and rarely a shared experience."

"How do you know all this?" Olga said, an accusation more than a question.

Gracie stared down at Olga's slightly raised sword. "We learn about this city's history as part of our education."

"And you know it's true?"

"As much as I can say anything I've been taught is true. There are very few facts that haven't been tainted by bias." Gracie snapped her hands out to either side and pressed down on the air, forcing everyone to halt.

"Wha—"

"Shh!" Gracie cut Olga off.

His friends as confused as him, it took William a few seconds before he heard it. Maybe Gracie's time in the city had sharpened her senses.

The uneven beat of footsteps. The slathering grunt of phlegm-clogged lungs. A diseased lolloped past the café, and Hawk bristled, but Gracie shoved him back. The moon highlighted the creature's twisted and galloping form. On the edge of its balance, it fell from one step into the next and stared straight ahead as if it had somewhere to be, streaking across the front of the café before vanishing from sight.

William's tight grip sweated on Jezebel's handle.

"How did—"

A raised finger halted Max mid-sentence. After another ten seconds, Gracie finally broke the silence. "That's one of the many reasons we pass through this place at night. The shadows are our friend. If the diseased don't see or hear us, then we don't have to fight them."

"Duh!" Olga said.

"*You* didn't hear it coming," William said.

Olga scowled at him.

Matilda spoke in a whisper. "Are there many diseased in the city?"

A shake of her head, Gracie then hooked a thumb to show

them their intended destination through the other side of the café. "You rarely get swarms of them. Fear and Fury do a good job of thinning their numbers. Now let's move."

Two metal frames were all that remained of the café's front doors. They followed Gracie's path through them, small pieces of glass popping beneath their steps.

Gracie's long ginger plait flicked one way and then the other when she looked up and down the next road.

William shivered and hugged himself for warmth. The street had a bank of buildings on either side that funnelled the wind, condensing its blast.

"On my count, I need you to follow me," Gracie said. "One … two … three …"

Gracie took off, running with a slight stoop across the road, Artan behind her, followed by Dianna, Matilda, Olga, Max, and finally William.

From the other side of the road, their destination had looked like a dark pit, but now they were closer, William saw the steep steps leading down into a tunnel.

"Fuck no!" Olga said. And who could blame her? She halted and shook her head. "No way am I going down there. No fucking way."

Gracie shrugged and descended into the darkness. The others followed her.

When William placed a hand on Olga's back, she snapped taut, and her grip on her sword tightened. "What else do you propose we do?" he said.

"I don't care, but I'm not going down there."

"So you're going to stay up here and wait for another diseased to find you?"

"I'm *not* going down there. I don't trust her."

"Or you're scared?"

An ugly twist to her face, Olga said, "Of course I'm fucking scared. Look at where we're going."

"So, what? We leave you?"

"Do what you want. I'm not going down there."

"You need to let this whole Gracie thing go. Other than her and Max being friends, you have no reason to hate her."

"I don't trust her." A sharp shake of her head, Olga said. "Besides, it's nothing to do with her and Max."

"Right."

"I'll say it again … *look* at where she wants us to go."

But if William stared into the darkness for too long, he wouldn't go down there either. From where he stood, the moonlight revealed only a small part of the tunnel. How many steps would it be before they were utterly blind? How deep did they have to go? "But you don't like her."

"What's that got to do with anything?"

"*Everything.* It impairs your judgement."

"One of us has to question her motives lest she lead us all to our deaths. You need me to keep the Gracie fan club grounded."

Maybe she had a point. Another biting gust of wind cut into William. "I'm sorry, Olga, but I won't let your jealousy put me in danger."

"Fuck you, William."

William took the steps two at a time. Made from the grey stone Gracie had called concrete, the edges of the stairs were wrapped with metal as if to protect against corrosion. So far, it had worked.

The darkness of the tunnel stretched away from them like one of the asylum's unlit corridors. Max paced in small circles, spinning his war hammer in a two-handed grip. It took for him to make three to four laps before he halted and looked William up and down. "Where's Olga?"

William held up both of his hands, his fingers splayed. He counted down from ten, starting with the little finger on his right hand.

With three fingers remaining, the tap of Olga's footsteps called down to them, marking her descent. Her scowl might have been aimed at Gracie, but if she saw it, she did a good job pretending she hadn't. Gracie set off at a jog into the darkness.

The moonlight shone down the stairs behind them. Not as dark as it had looked from the street. They ran past small booths on either side of the tunnel. Each one had a metal shutter pulled down in front of it. Each one bolted into the ground. Although, every one of them had been mangled from where they'd been prized away to create openings large enough for someone to climb through. The small shops had been looted a long time ago.

William ran at the back, Olga and Max ahead of him. For the acid in her words when she spoke to Gracie, a different Olga spurred Max on with kind encouragement.

Gracie halted when they reached the end of the line of shops. The group fell in behind her.

"I let her go," Max said.

The group turned his way, all of them taking this chance to catch their breath.

"Monica," he said. "I let Monica go."

"You what?" Gracie shook her head. "You saw what she did to everyone, right?"

Olga stepped towards the girl leading them. "He was on the receiving end of some of it. And you did fuck all about it."

"That's not fair, Olga." Max shook his head. "There was nothing Gracie could have done. She helped me when she could. I nearly got *her* killed." After a moment's silence, he said, "I felt sorry for Monica. She was so broken. She'd spent years in that dark and horrible place. She never knew when she'd get her next meal. *If* she'd get her next meal. She'd completely lost track of time. She's lived with that for longer than I've been alive. Imagine that."

Gooseflesh pinched the back of William's neck. The tunnels they were in were too similar to those in the asylum. Imagine twenty years in a place like this. Locked up. Abused …

Gracie's tone softened. "But what if she goes back to the asylum or the palace?"

Max had stepped back a pace, deeper into the shadows. He shook his head. "I watched her die," he finally said. "She said she'd rather have a minute of freedom. She knew she had no place in the new community, so she ran. She ran across the meadow and got taken down by diseased. I felt like she deserved that choice."

Max flinched when William reached out and touched him. "This isn't the asylum, Max. We're safe here. We don't have to listen to people's suffering." The shake running through Max's frame to William's grip suggested he nodded.

A dull light came on, temporarily blinding William.

Gracie stood up from the switch.

Max quickly wiped his eyes, but the glistening tracks remained on his cheeks. Other than William, no one else seemed to have noticed. Instead, they stared at what lay ahead.

"What the …?" Matilda said.

Chunky metal stairs stretched away from them down into another tunnel.

"We're going deeper?" Olga said.

Matilda pointed down the stairs. "At least we can see where we're going."

The large stairs had sharp, right-angled edges lined with small spikes. They looked like cogs in a giant machine.

"What the hell is this place?" Artan said.

"The armies that fight one another in the city," Gracie said, "rarely come down here, especially at night." She pointed down the stairs.

William and the others stepped closer to see the pile of bodies at the bottom.

"And very few of the diseased have the coordination to deal with these stairs without falling and killing themselves."

"I can see why," Olga said.

"This is the safest way through the city. At least for part of the journey. Unfortunately, it doesn't take us to our destination."

Gracie stepped down, the *tock* of her first step striking the top stair like a hammer blow.

Where the others froze, William shoved his way through and went next. Handrails on either side, they were rough with perished rubber. He used them to stabilise himself.

The *tock* of the others' footsteps, William focused on his path rather than behind. Hopefully, all of them were following him.

Close to the bottom, the sour reek of dead diseased curdled the air. The entire group were quietened by their concentration.

Olga finally said, "If this is the safest and least used route, why are there lights down here?"

"We don't know who originally fitted them," Gracie said. "Or who else knows about them. But we've used them for years and have never had a problem."

Olga might have had more questions, but Gracie had already set off again, jumping the diseased corpses and ducking into a tunnel on her right.

"This is a platform for a train station," Gracie said when the others joined her. "This is one mode of transport they used to get around." The large cylindrical vehicle in front of them had smashed windows. Small amounts of foam clung to some old seats inside, but they were mostly benches of bare metal. "The people of the city used to come all the way down here, queue on this platform, and then let this thing shuttle them to where they wanted to go."

Dianna's voice echoed when she leaned into the train. "Not one for the claustrophobic."

"Quite," Gracie said and stepped into the abandoned vehicle when Dianna pulled back out again.

William once again led the others, Matilda reaching ahead to thread her fingers through his. The string of lights continued into the train, giving them a path to follow. It shone on the brown stains of old blood on the floor. The deeper they ventured, the more stains they passed over.

"I thought you said it was safe down here?" Olga said.

"Safer," Gracie called back. "Nowhere's safe in this city. I thought I made that clear?"

"Great! So we're going to get slaughtered in a tunnel?"

"Not if you listen to me and follow my instructions."

The string of lights led them out of the train. The end of the massive cylindrical vehicle hung open, the metal peeled back like the shutters on the booths upstairs. About three feet to the ground, Gracie jumped down and landed with a crunch. William landed on the stones next. The train sat on two parallel tracks that ran away from them. Thick concrete sleepers every few feet kept the tracks level. Large grey stones filled the spaces in between.

"And no one comes down here?" William said.

"No." Gracie shook her head and leaned past him to watch Olga jump from the train last. She set off again. "It's too unpredictable. Especially at nighttime."

Their path laid out for them, William turned to look at the others, each of them frowning back at him. "But when the lights are on, surely it's fair game for anyone down here?"

Gracie dropped into a hunch, pulled several stones away, and killed the lights, throwing them into complete darkness.

Max whimpered.

The lights came back on and Gracie stood up. "We can turn them on and off as we please. The fact they've remained for as long as they have shows very few people have an interest in coming down here. But if we need to turn them off, we can. Now come on."

Max stood rigid. The wet tracks still shone on his cheeks.

William stepped towards him, but halted at the sound of footsteps. They called to them from down the tunnel. They moved fast. Faster than any of them could run. He readied Jezebel.

"Kill the lights, Gracie," Olga said, her hissed words laced with panic, her sword raised. "Turn the fucking lights off now!"

But Gracie ignored her.

"I told you we shouldn't trust her." Olga's voice grew louder. "She's a snake. She's set us up. I knew it!"

Gracie continued to ignore the fiery girl.

William stumbled when Olga shoved him in the back. "This is on you. You said we could trust her. Look where that's gotten us now. Why did we let you make the choices for us? We're going to fucking die down here because of her."

A relaxed frame, Gracie took slow steps towards the sound. The steps of someone meeting an old friend. The steps of someone in control. While the rest of them stood ready for war, she held her spear at her side. Had she sold them out? How could William have been such a terrible judge of character? After all they'd been through, had he just sentenced him and his friends to death? The word sat in his mouth like a spitball. But *sorry* wouldn't get them out of there. No matter how well he delivered his apology, it would mean absolutely nothing to dead cars.

CHAPTER 5

Olga clenched her teeth and growled, "I knew we shouldn't have trusted her."

The words turned through William, lifting his shoulders into his neck. *He* shouldn't have trusted her. He should have listened to Olga. But what could he say now? "Just shut up for a minute, yeah?"

"I will *not* be silenced, William. I will not take a slow and censored walk to my death because *you* can't see Gracie's an arsehole. If I have to make my own decisions to save my own life, then I will. But I like you and would prefer it if you came out of this alive too."

Gracie continued to walk away from them along the tunnel. A hand on the base of his back made William jump. Matilda stood behind him, her face pale in the weak light.

Quicker movement up ahead. Something ran towards Gracie. It slathered and panted, but it didn't run or sound like a diseased. It didn't have the clumsy and leaden-footed gait of their foetid predator. A diseased would have tripped and fallen on the uneven ground several times already. This thing moved fast and light of foot. William stepped back a pace. Jezebel already raised, he lifted her a little higher, ready to swing. The heavy weapon's lack of mobility would give him one chance. He'd have to make it count.

"What the …?" Artan said.

Gracie dropped into a hunch and laid her spear and knife on the large grey stones. She slipped the wrapped deer meat from her back and placed it on the ground.

"A dog?" Matilda said when the creature stepped into the light.

"And not just one," Dianna said.

More dogs followed. Six, eight, eleven of them, maybe more. Some of them were jet black and blended with the shadows.

Spasms fired up and down the length of William's legs, daring him to run. If these dogs turned, they wouldn't walk away from this encounter unscathed.

What appeared to be the biggest dog led the pack. Large enough that it could have stood on its hind legs and looked William in the eye. Covered in thick black fur, it had a white patch on its chest. It had a short nose and a square head. If that thing bit down, he'd have to drive a knife into its skull to detach it. Still six feet from Gracie, it dropped lower, its hackles raised in a stripe of fur along its back. It let out a low growl.

"There, there." Gracie spoke with a soft voice. "We're not here to fight you."

"I am!" Olga lunged forwards with her sword, and Hawk stepped forwards with her.

The lead dog skittered back several paces, retreating into the shadows. Its bared teeth shone in the darkness.

Olga spoke as if the creature and its pack understood her. "If any of those things come near me, they'll lose their heads."

"You're making it worse," Matilda said. "We're *all* scared."

"I'm not scared, I'm mad."

"It's the same thing."

When Olga settled down, Hawk doing the same a few seconds later, the lead dog returned its focus to Gracie. Its growl softened, but it remained hunched, displaying the coiled power in its muscly frame. For at least thirty seconds, the pair stood in a stalemate. A questioning of trust. Should the dog trust Gracie? Should anyone trust Gracie?

Gracie unwrapped the fabric, revealing the meat, before she slowly stood up and backed away. The entire pack of dogs watched her. When she'd retreated far enough, the alpha took a tentative step towards the package. The others waited.

William's heart pounded, tension turning through him. Even Olga kept her mouth shut. And a good job. Their chance to run had passed.

The lead dog sniffed the meat, tasted it with a lick, and then bit into it, pinning it with one of its enormous paws so it could tear a chunk free. As it backed off, chewing the deer meat, its dark eyes flitted from Gracie to the others while the rest of the pack piled in. A free-for-all, they fought one another for their chance at a meal.

Captivated by the feeding frenzy, the mass of densely packed bodies writhing, twisting, and competing with one another, it took for Gracie to hiss, "Come on," for William to see she'd retrieved her spear and knife and had moved to the far wall of the tunnel. "Let's get moving before they run out of food and we become more interesting to them again."

If any of the group had objections, they kept them to themselves. William led them after Gracie, Matilda directly behind him.

The dirty wall of the dark tunnel on their right, the group made their way past the pack on their left. The stones sloped away from the track. The angle proved difficult to walk along, the ground shifting beneath their steps. One or two of the dogs raised their heads. A small brown and black scruffy mutt watched them the entire way. The least threatening of the lot, yet it had the confidence of a lion.

The dogs snarled and growled with in-fighting as they scrapped to get their chance to eat. One or two of them yipped and pulled back. A snap of jaws. A loud bark. But they soon returned to the feast.

With the dogs behind them, Gracie quickened their pace.

Olga had been waiting for this moment. She said, "What the fuck—"

"Sing a different tune, Olga," Max said.

"Although," Matilda said, "she has a point. Gracie?"

The ginger girl turned to the group.

"What the hell was that all about?" Matilda said. "You could have given us a warning."

"If I gave you a warning for everything we might encounter in this city, we would have needed to stay in the ruined house for another week to cover it all."

Matilda shrugged. "So what was that about?"

"Dogs," Gracie said. When none of the group replied, she said, "Wild dogs live in these tunnels. They're mostly fine."

"Mostly?" Artan said.

"Look, would you rather take your chances with a pack of dogs who can be tamed, or the diseased?"

"It's a choice?" Hawk this time.

"It is. We don't know why, but the diseased don't like dogs. I mean, there are anomalies, but from what we've witnessed, they do what they can to avoid them. The very few that make it down here without killing themselves on the metal stairs try to get back out again the second they realise they have to share this space with dogs."

Hawk shook his spear. "The enemy of my enemy …"

"Exactly," Gracie said. "And they're quite sweet, really. We call the alpha Rocky."

"You've named it?" Olga said.

Gracie sighed. "Him. And what did you expect? That he'd name himself? You don't know much about dogs, do you, sweetie?"

Olga bit down on her bottom lip and raised her middle finger at Gracie.

Gracie led them around the next bend. "This is a platform," she said. A walkway similar to the one they'd seen at the other end, but no train this time. She laid her spear on the platform and used both hands to boost herself up. She reached back down and offered William a hand so he could follow. "It's where the people used to wait for the trains to arrive."

Between them, William and Gracie gave a hand up to everyone who wanted it. All of them, save Olga, who scrambled up by herself. Any dignity she'd hoped to retain slipped away with her kicking legs, her slithering on her belly, and her grunting as she dragged herself to her feet.

This journey mirrored the one down there. A different station, but they ducked through another archway and came to another flight of metal stairs leading up away from them. Another mound of broken, diseased bodies gathered at the bottom. Their foul reek tainted the air with the same acrid tang. Palpable, it clung to William's sweating skin and weaved into the fabric of his clothes.

They crossed the decomposing diseased one step at a time, testing their footing before they committed. William's knuckles ached with how tightly he gripped Jezebel. How did they know all the diseased in this pile were deceased?

The steep climb up the metal stairs pulled on the back of William's tired legs.

A red-faced and sweating Olga took up the rear. She reached the top of the stairs last. Gracie hovered nearby.

When Olga stepped clear, she said, "You didn't have to wait for me."

"I did." Gracie reached a hand down the side of the stairs, winced as she buried her arm deep into the metal frame, and, after a few seconds of searching around, turned the lights off with a *click!*

The darkness gave the moon its chance to shine again. A splash of silver light leaked down from the streets above, highlighting the small flight of stairs out of there. Once again, Gracie led the way.

William caught up to Gracie before she left the station and said, "Why did we go through there? Why not just go overground?"

"A pack of dogs isn't a big risk. Especially when you have cooked deer meat for them. We're almost certain to avoid the diseased for that section of our journey if we go the way we did, and there's a good chance we won't run into the soldiers either."

William climbed the stairs at Gracie's side, but before they stepped clear of the station, she threw her right arm across him and halted him mid-step. She pulled him back down into the shadows.

The others waited behind them in the train station and held their collective breaths. Even Olga had fallen silent. All of them had fixed on the man no more than fifty feet away.

CHAPTER 6

One man. Although, not really a man. A man like William had been a man when he'd gone on national service. A man in responsibility only. A man when someone needed bodies to perform duties, like build a wall or go into battle. A man to make it sound like he'd made his own choice to fight for the cause, to take part in a war that will never end. He wore blue trousers that looked like they were part of a uniform. A uniform that had been torn from him. He'd been left naked from the waist up. A sharp crease ran down the front of each trouser leg. At least they dressed them nicely before they sent them to be slaughtered. The trousers were dark. They glistened with the man's blood and probably a lot more besides. William leaned close to Gracie, keeping his voice low. "That's one of the soldiers?"

She nodded. "Fear wear blue. Fury wear red."

The boy hung chained between two vertical steel poles about twenty feet apart. The poles stood fifteen feet tall and had large glass spheres on top. How they'd remained intact for so long … In the past, the spheres would have glowed, lighting the city at night. The chains had been tied around the boy's ankles and wrists, stretching him into a star and suspending him like a fly caught in a web. His head hung limp, his weak, hairless torso rocking with his exhausted breaths.

Matilda spoke in a whisper. "What have they done to him?"

"They're bleeding him out," Gracie said.

"You've seen this done before?"

Gracie shrugged. "Variations of it, yes. They would have cut deep into the back of both of his thighs before tying him up for everyone to see."

Hawk appeared behind them and said, "Jeez!" his voice shooting out into the city.

Gracie pressed her finger to her lips. "Shh!"

Although he spoke with the breathy hiss of an attempted whisper, Hawk hadn't lowered his volume. He pointed at the boy. "He's still alive. Surely we need to do something?"

"There's nothing we can do to help him." Gracie shook her head. "Even if we do free him, he's already dead."

"So we just leave him?"

"Hawk, when I said you need to trust me, I didn't mean some of the time. You need to trust *every one* of my decisions."

"What is this, a dictatorship?" Olga said.

"Exactly!" Hawk had grown even louder.

"Will you keep your damn voice down?" Gracie stamped her foot.

Hawk climbed the stairs. He stood just inches from Gracie, who raised her chin in defiance.

William jumped when the hunter burst away from the group, charging towards the street.

With one swing of the blunt end of her spear, Gracie

cleaned out Hawks' feet. His shins bore the brunt of his fall, slamming against the stairs' metal edges.

Hawk rolled over onto his back. His face twisted as he coiled his right leg, showing Gracie the sole of his boot. But before he could connect with his attack, William kicked his foot away, redirecting his strike into the metal handrail attached to the wall beside them.

Hawk stood up and launched himself at William. He hit him in the chest, shoulder first, driving both of them back into the station.

The fall winded William, and before he could find his bearings, Hawk climbed on top of him and raised his right fist.

Max, Olga, and Matilda jumped in. They each took a limb, leaving William to grab the leg he'd diverted from striking Gracie. They restrained the wild hunter like the boy in the street above.

The others helped, all of them dragging a kicking and twisting Hawk deeper into the train station.

Possessed with a strength that proved a match for them all, Hawk continued to fight and turn. Hissing and spitting, he shook and writhed. He grunted through clenched teeth, his voice echoing in the enclosed space.

"Shut up!" Gracie hissed.

Hawk drew a breath to scream again, but before it left his mouth, Olga let go of his arm and drove a right cross into his chin. The *crack* of the connection rivalled any noise Hawk could have made, and the hunter fell limp.

Her fist still balled, Olga panted like the rest of them, standing over Hawk as if daring him to come around. She eventually looked at Gracie, her teeth gritted, her nostrils flared. Gracie dipped her a nod she didn't return.

William and the others went back to the stairs. "What are

we waiting for?" he said. "Not that I agree with Hawk's methods, but surely we have to do something? Let him down at least. The kid needs our help."

Gracie shook her head. "This isn't our war."

"Since when do we turn our back on suffering like that?"

William followed Gracie's line of sight. At first it looked like shifting shadows. A trick of the light, even. But then the scenery came to life. The hunched and scrawny form of a man stepped into the road. Long hair, a long beard, and so skinny he looked like a skeleton with skin. His clothes hung from him in rags, and the moonlight showed he only had a few teeth remaining in his mouth.

He sniffed the air as if guided towards the restrained soldier by scent.

"It's always just a matter of time before the scavengers turn up," Gracie said. "Had Hawk rushed out, they would have seen us. Believe me, you don't want to be fighting them if you can avoid it."

"Whose side are they on?" Dianna said.

"No one's." Gracie shook her head. "They live in the city. They get by however they can."

Something in the way she said it turned William's blood cold. *However they can.*

His movements erratic like that of a diseased, the scavenger's arms twitched, spasms snapping through him. He giggled to himself.

More shifting in the shadows, several more scavengers emerged as if birthed from the surrounding buildings. How did they hide themselves so well? Men and women, some of them children as young as nine or ten. At least ten to fifteen of them. They formed a semicircle around the suspended soldier.

As if buoyed by the support of his peers, the scrawny man

burst to life. He closed the final few feet between him and the soldier. He turned one way and then the other as if spooked by his surroundings. On his third erratic shift, he fixed on a large lump of rubble, skipped to it, and giggled as he dragged it back to the boy. He stepped up onto the lump of concrete so he stood at the same height as the soldier.

A check over each shoulder again. The scavenger's crew remained close by. He grabbed the soldier's hair and lifted his limp head. Eyeball to eyeball with the boy, he leaned so close their noses touched. He giggled the entire time.

Several of the older males in the group clicked their tongues. The sharp cracks whipped through the abandoned streets.

The scavenger on the lump of rubble poked the boy's face. Was he testing him? Seeing if he'd suddenly burst to life?

This seemed to satisfy the others, who closed in. The children and women replaced the tongue-clicks with a low hum. They continued to hold back, their tone increasing in volume.

"What are they going to do to him?" Artan said.

One of the older males stepped forwards. The one on the rubble jumped clear. The group's scout, he made sure everything was safe for the elders. The older male carried a blade, the glint of it catching the moonlight. He stepped up onto the rubble and sawed into the soldier's bicep.

The soldier dragged a breath in through his clenched teeth. His chest swelled and his eyes rolled in a battle for consciousness. He yelled when the elder made a second cut.

But the strength left the soldier, blood raining down from his wound as the elder held up a strip of wet flesh. A slug of human anatomy. He held it over his open mouth in a pinch before letting it fall.

Blood ran over the elder's lips and chin as he turned to face the others while he chewed on the soldier.

All the while, the women and children hummed.

The elder jumped from the rock to make space for the scout. The next one to feed. He now also had a blade in his hand.

As the scout cut into the boy's stomach, Dianna barked with an effort to suppress a heave and stumbled away down the stairs.

Her steps heavy, she ran into the darkness, retching as she vanished. The splash of vomit hit the tiled floor far enough away to not attract the scavengers' attention.

Before the scout feasted on his cut of flesh, William and the others followed Dianna back into the station. A thick tang of vomit hung in the air.

It took a few seconds for William's stomach to settle. "You never told us about them," he said to Gracie.

"I've already told you, there's a lot to know about this city, and I haven't had time to explain it all."

Olga threw her arms wide, the slap of them hitting her sides when they came back down again. "And you didn't think the scavengers might have been worth mentioning? And if not, what the fuck else are we going to run into that you've not told us about?"

"I'm not withholding information," Gracie said.

"You are." Matilda this time.

"But I've already said, if I held a Q and A about what lies ahead, we would have been on the edge of the city for another week. Look, this is the last time I'll offer this; if you want to go back, I'll help you return to the edge of the city." She pointed towards the scavengers. "When I get to the top of those stairs, I'm not turning around. I can't promise you what we'll come across, but I can promise you I'll do my best to make sure you're safe. *If* you listen to me."

Hawk remained unconscious, lying on his back on the train station's dirty tiled floor.

"One thing I'm pretty certain of, is you'll witness some more awful things before we're out of the other side of this place. But I've done this enough times to be confident we can get through. You need to decide what you want to do."

As one, the group turned to look at William. Even Olga.

CHAPTER 7

If they wanted to get south of the wall, the easiest and most efficient way would be to pass through the city. William had seen one of the walled communities bordering the ruins, and if Gracie had told them the truth, another one sat on the other side. Surely, using the abandoned buildings as cover had to be their best chance of getting through unnoticed. They'd stand out from a mile away if they tried to travel across open land. When William put that to the group, none of them objected.

They gave Hawk the time he needed to recover from Olga's punch and to then apologise for being a moron. While they waited in the train station's darkness, the soldier's screams ended, and the chains rattled from where they untied him and took his body away.

The moon created more shadows than light. Danger could have been hiding in the darkness, but they couldn't let unseen enemies halt their progress. They stepped from the station onto a wide road, the asphalt streaked with cracks packed with dense clumps of grass.

They were all on a strict order to only talk when essential. Questioning Gracie's choices didn't count as essential. Not that it stopped Olga trying every time they slowed down.

William ran directly behind Gracie and became a shield between her and the others. He matched her pace, locking into a steady rhythm as he followed her through another window of an old building. Glass crunched and popped beneath their steps. Wrecks of tables and chairs filled the space like in the café earlier. A large metal block sat over to their right, its flat top stained black and covered in dirt.

"This used to be a restaurant," Gracie said. "They cooked food on that thing over there."

William nodded. "I'm sure it was much easier than building a fire." He checked behind. The others remained close.

Gracie halted immediately after jumping through another window. William hopped through and landed beside her. Another wide road. The city appeared to conform to a grid layout. Unlike the ruins outside Edin, where the streets were all different shapes and sizes, made from different materials from concrete to large stones, this city had the appearance of one designed and built from scratch rather than added to over time.

They were now just twenty feet from the first of the three tall towers. To look up them hurt the base of William's neck, and his head spun.

"No fucking way," Olga said.

Gracie shot her a hard glare and pressed her finger to her lips. How many times did she have to tell her?

But it didn't silence the small firecracker. Instead, she attempted a whisper. "No way am I going in there. I'm not climbing to the top of those towers. You're showing off now." Her face glistened with sweat, and she fought to regulate her breathing as if battling against a rising panic attack. She gulped and shook her head. "No way."

And she didn't have to. But Gracie shrugged and darted across the road in the tower's direction. Olga could find her own way.

The group looked to William again. Who did he back? He had no reason to doubt Gracie. He looked both ways and charged across the road to the first tower's entrance.

Like almost every other building in the city, the large rotating doors lacked the glass they would have once had. And a good job, because the top and bottom wore a rash of rust that suggested they wouldn't turn no matter how hard they shoved. William stepped through the metalwork into the vast foyer, the remains of a wooden desk directly in front of them. The black tiled floor leeched what little light made it inside. Although, the two entrances in the far wall remained visible. One, a single doorway, minus the door that would have once filled it. The other, closed metal double doors. They were covered in rust and clearly hadn't been opened in years.

The rest followed William in, Olga taking up the rear.

"You ready?" Gracie said.

William shrugged and Olga said, "No."

Gracie set off again, leading them through the doorway with the missing door to a dark stairwell. Sets of ten to fifteen stairs before they turned one hundred and eighty degrees and ran up another flight. The shadows made it impossible to see all the way to the top. William's words ran ahead of him, those too dying in the gloom. "How high are we going?"

"We're going to the top."

"You're taking the piss," Olga said.

"I wish I were." Again, Gracie gave them no time to argue.

They moved quickly, their collective steps rolling like

thunder. William's head spun every time he turned to climb the next flight. His legs on fire, his lungs working at full capacity. He caught a foot several times where he'd not lifted his leg high enough. He carried Jezebel with both hands.

Just before William could ask Gracie to stop, she paused, a window letting in enough light to reveal a large number ten on the wall.

William rested Jezebel on his knees, leaned over the handle, and pulled in deep breaths. "Can—" he paused for breath "—we—" breathe "—slow the—" breathe "—pace a little?"

Gracie hadn't even broken a sweat. Dianna hadn't either. Who knew? Gracie's features played out as if she had difficulty finding sympathy for his struggle, but she finally shrugged and said, "Okay, let's walk for a while."

At the eleventh floor, William halted again. A long corridor stretched away from them. It had doors lining either side. "What did this place used to be?"

"It was both a hotel and office space."

"What are they?" Matilda said.

"A hotel is where people came to stay for a few nights and paid for the privilege. An office is a place where businesses operated."

"Like insurance?" Artan said with a smile.

"Exactly. And redundant now."

Artan's face fell slack. "Cyrus would have loved to see this place."

Olga snorted a laugh. "And he would have crapped his pants to be in here."

After a few seconds, Artan smiled and nodded. "Yeah, you're probably right."

They stopped next when they reached the twentieth floor. Another window without a pane. The wind howled, stinging William's eyes when he looked out over the city.

They were higher than most of the surrounding buildings. "Are we at the halfway point yet?"

"We're past halfway," Gracie said.

William's clothes itched from where they clung to his sweating body. "I've never been this far from the ground in my life."

Gracie laughed. "Wait 'til you get to the top."

At the twenty-first floor, William halted again, the others stopping behind him.

Gracie halted a few steps later, threw her arms out to the sides, and came back down to him. "What is it?"

William pointed through a doorway. A corridor like they'd seen on many other floors, but this one had the remains of a fire in it. He might have missed it completely were it not for the moonlight catching the streaks of white where bones lay amongst the charred lumps. Bones that could have been human.

"Scavengers?" Hawk said, stepping towards the corridor. Olga grabbed him and tugged him back.

Gracie nodded. "I'd say so. Although, they look to be long—"

A gust of wind hit William in the back and shot past him down the corridor. It blew the ash away from the top of the fire. The embers beneath glowed red.

"You were saying?" Olga said. She kept a hold of Max.

Lowering her voice to a whisper, Gracie hooked a thumb over her shoulder. "Come on, let's keep moving."

They broke into a jog again, their steps louder with their haste.

Maybe William imagined it, but every time they passed a new floor, he glanced in and glimpsed someone there. A silhouette or two in the shadows. But on every second check, they'd gone. Tricks of the light? Ghosts? Scavengers?

Floor twenty-eight.

Floor twenty-nine.

They were just a few floors from the top. They followed Gracie past the large number thirty and up the next flight of stairs leading to a metal door. The old hinges groaned as she forced it wide.

William froze again, the others slamming into him. Had he just seen that? Several floors below, the dirty face of a scavenger peering up at them.

"Come on!" Matilda shoved William.

He must have imagined it. They were looking to him for guidance. The last thing he should do was panic about invisible enemies. He could tell them about it when they were well away from here.

The second William stepped out onto the roof, the wind shoved him back a pace. It burned his eyes and stung his skin. He dipped his head into the strong gales and moved aside to let the others through, each of them leaning forwards into the force of nature. All of them walked on weary legs. All of them save Gracie and Dianna.

"Wow," William said. "I know I said it earlier, but I've never been this high up." The trio of towers had been built close to one another. The drop to the ground made William's head spin. He stepped back, his heart in his throat.

Gracie placed a hand on the back of William's arm. "Give it a moment. You'll get used to it."

Several rounds of deep breaths, William returned to the edge. Still woozy, but his dizziness had left him. The city stretched away from them in every direction. The tops of the buildings were lit by the moon. There were older structures with spires that pointed at the sky. A vast metal arena, a webbing of rusting steel over its open roof. Seats surrounded a rectangular patch of mud. What had it once been? Did they use it for trials like with the national service area?

Ascetically ruined, but structurally sound, the buildings

might have looked a mess, but they were unlike anything William had seen before. It was like witnessing the future. A post-future. What if they rediscovered the secrets that had died with this society? What could they do with them now? The dark night prevented him from seeing to the edge of the city, let alone beyond it. How close were they to the wall? Did they have communities on either side of them like Gracie had said? If only he could come back here during the day.

"Now, while I think this is a wonderful trick," Olga said, stepping back from the building's edge, "has it really been necessary for us to come up this high?"

"Like when we went through the tunnel," Gracie said, "the less time we spend on the city's streets, the better." She pointed at a pile of thick hollow poles. They were made from brushed steel. Unlike the rest of the metal William had seen in this place, these were rust-free. They'd seen a lot of use. Several slipped and clanged when Gracie pulled one from the stack. A small lip about a foot tall ran around the edge of the roof. It had grooves cut into it every few feet. Gracie laid one of the poles in one of the grooves and leaned it across the gap between the two buildings.

William's stomach flipped with how close she stood to the edge. One powerful gust could end her. Especially with the weight of the pole tipping her balance.

"No way." Artan this time. He shook his head and repeated, "No way am I climbing across that gap. No."

"Come on, Gracie." The aggression had left Olga's voice. "Surely there's no need for this?"

But Gracie went back for the next pole. Before she lifted it, the metal door leading from the stairs flung wide with a *crack!*

A short woman with wild and greasy black hair. The face that had stared up at William. She charged at them. Her toothless mouth stretched wide in a scream. She wielded a metal bar and ran straight at Olga.

Hawk released a yell to rival the woman's. His spear in one hand, his knife raised, he charged at her. But he tripped, fell hard, landed on his shoulder, and cleared Olga's legs from beneath her.

Gracie intercepted the scavenger before she reached the fallen pair. She grabbed her ragged shirt and turned away from her, using the woman's momentum to launch her over her shoulder. The woman's scream changed in pitch as she flew in an arc over the side of the building.

William led the charge to the edge, the others joining him. He dropped to his knees and held onto the building's raised brickwork lip. It stopped his head spinning. The scavenger's arms and legs flailed as she fell.

She hit the ground with a loud *kaboom!* The explosion shook the building, and a ball of fire engulfed the dead woman. It swirled on the ground and turned into a sphere of acrid smoke that rose and slammed into William's face.

"Those," Gracie said, "are landmines. They are lots of them in this part of the city. You can see many of them from where the road's been torn to shreds."

A jagged line ran through the churned road between the two towers like an angry scar.

"But some of them are hidden. We don't know how the mines got there, but the more time you spend on the ground, the more likely you are to step on one. Especially in the dark. Maybe we're being overcautious using the roofs of these buildings, but it's the safest route we've found." She turned to Olga. "You think we enjoy climbing this tower?" A shake of her head. "Not at all, but it is what it is. We want to be safe, and this is the only way to cross from one building to the next."

Gracie laid three more poles across the gap before she

tossed her spear to the roof of the next building, gripped onto one of the poles, and let herself swing around so she hung beneath it.

William's stomach lurched and the back of his knees tingled.

Her legs crossed at the ankles, Gracie shimmied over, apparently impervious to the effects of being so high. At the other side, she reached back and pulled herself onto the roof of the building opposite.

Fortunately, Matilda made a decision before William had to. She yanked Jezebel from his grip and threw it after Gracie. It landed on the flat roof on the other side. She followed Gracie's lead, shimmying across the pole. Like Gracie, she moved as if she'd done it a thousand times.

Now William needed to find the motivation to follow her.

CHAPTER 8

The cold pole and strong winds turned William's hands numb. His knuckles ached from his tight grip, and the wind slammed into him as he hung between the second and third tower. But he kept going. An inch at a time. He'd already crossed from the first to the second tower, so he could do it again. Besides, all the others had crossed as if they'd done it a thousand times, even Dianna, who'd been the meekest of the group since they'd liberated her from the asylum. Only Matilda had waited for him on the second building, offering him a back slap of encouragement for his first tentative crossing. She then scooted over to the final roof.

William looked down and damn near lost his stomach. His head spun. His grip weakened. He clung tighter to the frigid pole. Any tighter and he'd dislocate his knuckles. They'd break before the thick steel yielded, hollow or not.

The moon shone a spotlight on him. It made him easy to see from the dark windows running down the sides of the tower blocks. The wind played the tall buildings. Were there people inside waiting to spring an attack? Scavengers?

Diseased? Visible for everyone to see, he gave them every opportunity with how long this crossing had already taken. He nodded to himself and grunted through gritted teeth. "Come on, William. You can do it!"

About halfway between the towers, his jaw tight as if the strength of his clench could somehow allay the biting cold in the cutting wind. He looked down again. The line of windows showed him the way to the ground. He'd travel several hundred feet in a matter of seconds. Mines or not, the impact would shatter every bone in his body.

"William, sweetie." Matilda leaned from the edge of the tower. "Look at me." She smiled, but her eyes pinched at the sides. "You've got this, okay?"

Trembling, William nodded. He had this. He could do it.

William yelled when the metal pole slipped against the bricks. He clung to the bar, hugging it, the cold steel against his chest. But the movement hadn't come from him. Gracie pulled one of the spare poles free, dragging it across to the third tower's roof before laying it flat and moving on to the next one. It took her a few seconds to look at William. She clapped a hand to her mouth. "I'm so sorry. I should have warned you."

"You reckon?"

"We have to pull the poles back across. As long as we take them all the way with us, there's always some on either side. Sorry."

Sweat rose on William's brow and instantly turned cold in the biting wind. One hand over the other. An inch at a time. Like he'd done when crossing from the first to the second tower. He'd done it before. He'd do it again.

"That's it, William." Matilda remained at the edge of the roof. Just a few feet away. "You're nearly there. Keep going."

The last two feet were the hardest. The cold locked his hands into claws. Much more time on this bar and his grip would fail him. His muscles burned with fatigue, and he trembled. An inch at a time.

William threw his right hand back, slamming his knuckles against the edge of the roof. The salt in his sweating skin burned the fresh graze. A countdown in his head. Three, two, one. He threw his right hand back again. This time he caught the inside edge of the lip of brickwork around the top of the tower. He pulled himself towards the building.

Hands reached over and grabbed his clothes. Matilda and Gracie, they pulled him towards the roof, his shoulder blades scraping over the rough bricks. He fell over the other side of the lip, landing cheek first on the roof's gravelled surface.

Gasping and lying on his back, William closed his eyes. When he opened them, Matilda looked down on him with a wide grin. "Well done! You did it."

"Will you ever let me forget about this?"

"What do you mean?"

"Will this be like the time in Edin when I tried to make a jump and fell?"

Matilda laughed. "You're still bitter about that?" She leaned in and kissed him. "Well done. I'm proud of you."

A few seconds to gather himself, William remained on his back and stared up at the half-moon.

Gracie dragged the final pole across with a scrape. It pinged as she laid it with the others. She offered William her hand.

Up on shaking legs, the wind rocking his fatigued form as if it blew stronger than before. William retrieved Jezebel and walked to the edge of the roof. The city stretched away from them. "How long before we're out of this place?"

"I reckon an hour," Gracie said. "Keep doing as I say and we'll make it."

"Unless we see a better route ourselves," Olga said.

Gracie had taken to pretending she didn't hear Olga. For

the best, really. There seemed little point in engaging in an argument neither would back down from.

"See that tall tower over there?" Gracie pointed, and it took William a few seconds to pick out the large metal structure against the dark sky. Triangular in shape, it started with a wide base and narrowed to a point. Not as tall as the tower they stood on, but taller than many of the buildings surrounding it. She said, "That's where we're heading."

William traced a line with his eyes from the bottom of the tower to their destination. The enormous arena stood in their way. "Uh," he said, "will we go through that thing?"

"The stadium?" Gracie said. She nodded. "Yeah, it's the best route. Like with the buildings and the roofs, there aren't any mines in the stadium because the diseased don't go through there."

"You know"—Olga said it so loud William jumped—"I would have beaten that scavenger on the roof back there." She pointed at the first tower. A dark glare levelled on Hawk. Her eyes narrowed. "If *he* hadn't tried to be a hero and tripped me over while he was at it."

Aimed at Gracie, the red-headed girl opened her mouth to reply, but Olga cut her off.

"What I'm saying is I didn't need your help."

"I never said you did. And you're right, Hawk made it a lot harder. Maybe next time"—she turned to the stocky hunter—"let Olga fight her own battles."

"The same could be said to you," Olga said.

A long intake of breath raised Gracie's chest before she deflated with her exhalation. "So that's the plan. We need to get to that tower. Does anyone have questions?"

They all turned to Olga. Thankfully, she didn't.

"Everyone okay to move on?" Gracie said. "I don't know about you lot, but I'm ready to get out of this city. And we definitely need to be out of here before day breaks. This place gets lively then."

William bounced on his toes and shook his hands to work the aches from his arms. When no one else protested, Gracie set off for the metal door leading into the building.

CHAPTER 9

Like with every old steel door William had encountered, the hinges on the one leading to the tower's stairwell groaned and cackled when Gracie pulled it wide. The echo of the mocking call ran down into the darkness. Thankfully, nothing replied.

His body still weak with spent adrenaline, William held back and let the others in ahead of him before he followed Matilda into the building. Jezebel in one hand, he caught the closing door with his other, easing it shut to keep the noise down, and reducing the already poor visibility.

The stairwell had one window every few floors. They let in enough splashes of light to reveal their path in stages. They became illuminated checkpoints, each one taking them ever closer to their way out of the abandoned tower.

Gracie led the line. Too far away for William to hear the details of her conversation, but he got the gist when she turned on Olga with a finger to her lips and hissed, "Shh!"

Olga stepped back a pace, showing Gracie her palms in defence.

William picked his steps carefully, the light from the last

window and the glow from the next not enough to guide him. He placed each foot before moving on. If he fell, his weak body would turn him into a rag doll, and he wouldn't stop until he hit the bottom step.

Despite Gracie's warning, Olga's mutterings started up again. He still couldn't hear the details, but from the tension in Gracie's back, and from the unrelenting jabbering, he could make a good guess. Another slew of dissent. Another line of questioning that challenged the ginger girl's right to lead them.

"Will you shut the fuck up?" Gracie said. Louder this time.

"No, I won't." Olga placed her balled hands on her hips. "I won't let—"

Gracie grabbed Olga by the front of her shirt with one hand and the back of the head with the other. She turned the girl ninety degrees, forcing her to look into the long corridor beside them. The number on the wall told them they were on the twenty-first floor.

The moonlight shone through the paneless hole that had once been a window on this floor. Whatever Gracie had just shown Olga, it stole both her words and her will to fight.

Artan next, he poked his head through the doorway, glancing back up at Matilda with tightened lips and raised eyebrows. Hawk, Dianna, and Max all did the same, although none of them shared their concern with Matilda. Instead, they redoubled their efforts towards their silent escape, moving down the stairs on tiptoes at a quickened pace.

After Matilda had looked through the doorway, William leaned in. A long corridor like they'd seen on every other floor. Doors on either side. But this time, bodies spilled from the rooms. Tens of bodies. Had they been slaughtered? One of them twitched and snorted as she inhaled before she rolled onto her side. A headless and limbless torso lay in the corridor about fifteen feet away. Half-eaten and covered in its own blood, it glistened in the moonlight. The soldier they'd seen the scavengers take earlier? Hard to tell.

Another one of them grunted. A directionless kick snapped through her leg. William pulled back. No wonder Olga had shut up. Where the torso came from didn't matter. They couldn't help the person now. They simply needed to get out of the building without being heard.

Maybe they moved with the same amount of stealth as before, but every gentle step on the concrete stairs now went off like an exploding mine. Which one would disturb the sleeping mob above? How much of a head start would they need to get away safely?

They passed the eighth floor before Olga started again. "Yet another thing you chose not to mention."

"Olga," Max said. One of the few things he'd said since they'd buried Cyrus.

A softening of her features, Olga turned Max's way.

"Will you shut the fuck up and let Gracie lead us out of here?"

Olga drew a breath to reply, but this time she caught it before it passed her lips. As the threat of her response died, some of William's tension left his upper body.

"Besides," Gracie said, "you saw how Hawk behaved on the roof when he felt the need to be a hero." The hunter's face reddened while Gracie addressed him directly. "Thankfully, there was only one of them. The last thing we need is him planning to go to war against an army. It's better he doesn't know where they are."

∽

Since they'd entered this city, the moon hadn't shone bright enough for their needs. But now William stepped from the dark stairwell, the silver glare dazzled him. He rubbed his stinging eyes before looking up the length of the tall tower. Lines of windows ran all the way to the roof. The tallest building he'd ever seen, it appeared even taller since he'd looked from the top down. Not only could he gauge the climb, but he now also had a better sense of the fall.

The wind continued to whistle through the gaps in this tower and many around them. Just another ruined building. As abandoned as all the others in the city. How could they know what slept on the twenty-first floor if they hadn't witnessed it? How could they know what resided inside any of the structures? Thank the heavens they had Gracie as their guide. They'd be dead without her.

"You all ready?" Gracie said.

The nods passed all the way down to William, who shrugged his compliance. He took off after the others, led by Gracie across the wide road.

A row of one-storey buildings on the other side of the street. They'd once been stores of some sort. Gracie boosted from a window ledge, caught the roof of one, and pulled herself up.

Some of William's strength had returned, as if having his feet on the ground revitalised him.

All the others took a path to the roof. Max managed it with the least effort. He threw his war hammer up ahead of him, kicked from the window ledge, and pulled himself up without breaking stride. William did the same with Jezebel.

Gracie had already set off across the flat rooftops, Olga on her tail. The small firecracker refused to be beaten or left behind, even if it killed her.

Some of the buildings had gaps between them of only a few feet. William retrieved Jezebel, held her with one hand, and took them in his stride, chasing after Matilda like he used to when they ran through Edin. And like when they ran through Edin, she moved as if she'd been born on a high wire. Her lightness of foot, her grace and balance, she flew across the rooftops with soundless steps.

Several shops ahead of William, Gracie halted and lowered into a hunch. Olga followed suit. Hawk, Max, Dianna, Artan, and then Matilda did the same. William dropped just in time, the snarling fury of the diseased charging past them on the road down to their left. They were on a mission, their crimson glares fixed on a point in the distance. As oblivious to William and his friends as they were to the scavengers and sentries undoubtedly watching them from the shadows. The pack's snarling and hissing faded, and William lifted his head. Hopefully, they'd run into a mine.

Gracie took off again, jumping from the last shop to the ground and tearing across the next cracked road.

The jolt of William's landing snapped through his body, but he didn't have time to manage the aches. Matilda, as the next closest to him, had already reached the halfway point in the road. He gritted his teeth and chased after her.

The stadium loomed large. Another feat of engineering unlike any he'd encountered. Imagine what it had looked like full. Imagine being a protector, slaying the diseased in front of thousands of spectators.

Metal stairs ran up the outside of the stadium. The others reached them, their feet beating a tattoo against the steps until they reached a part with a section missing. Three or four stairs had fallen victim to corrosion. Gracie cleared the space, the gap meaningless. Olga, not to be beaten, followed next.

The others all made it look easy. Weapons in hand, they leaped as if certain of landing. Lactic acid burned William's calves.

Matilda cleared the gap, taking it in her stride. But he didn't jump like her; they both knew that. When Matilda stopped to check on him, William slowed down. He didn't need an audience.

"I believe in you," Matilda said.

William leaped from the first broken stair too early. Only one hand free, Jezebel in the other. White-hot agony slammed into his shins as he landed across the edge of the next step. Nausea gripped his stomach and clamped his testicles. Sweat lifted on his brow. He clung to the stairs with a shaking hand.

Matilda locked a tight grip over the back of his wrist. She had him, but she gave him a moment before she helped him back to his feet. A smile he hadn't seen in a while lit her features. "Well done." His heart swelled when she kissed his cheek. "Now come on, hopefully it won't be long before we're at Gracie's community."

More grazes, William's shins stung from where he sweated into them. He stumbled up the remainder of the zigzagged staircase. At the top, the roof stretched away as a vast expanse of white corrugated steel. The webbing of rusting bars over their heads, he followed the others across the oval stadium.

Gracie, Olga, Dianna, Hawk, Max, and then Matilda all vanished through a torn hole in the corrugated roof. William held Jezebel down for Max to take before he lowered himself and dropped.

Thousands of blue sun-bleached plastic seats ran away from them in both directions. Gracie perched on one, her face glistening with sweat. Max and Dianna had sat down too, Artan standing next to Matilda while Olga twitched, ready to run again. The oval encompassed a muddy rectangle in the centre. The place would hold twenty thousand spectators. Maybe more. Hard to tell. "How many people lived in this city?"

"Hundreds of thousands," Gracie said, her chest rising and falling with her heavy breaths.

As they all recovered, William walked down the concrete stairs leading to the edge of the pitch. The echoes of dead dreams in his mind, thousands of spectators cheered him. He spoke beneath his breath. "Ladies and gentlemen, boys and girls, please be upstanding for the greatest protector Edin has ever seen. They thought Magma was good until this boy bested him as a teenager, exposing him for the fraud he was. Now you have a new hero. A protector worthy of the name and your trust. Someone who will do right by you and the city. Someone who loves Edin's residents and will die for them. The people's champion. The fiercest slayer the world has ever seen. Let me hear it for Spiiiiiiiiiiiike—"

"Dreams don't die easily, eh?"

William jumped and spun around.

Matilda grinned at him.

Heat flushed his cheeks, and his throat tightened. "Uh-uh-um …"

For the second time today, she smiled like she meant it. She reached out and held both of William's hands in her own. "The life of a protector wasn't for me, but I loved every ounce of your passion. I love your passion. What you've done to get us this far is greater than the work of any protector."

"W-what I've done?" William pulled in a dry gulp.

"Whether you like it or not, you've led us through this mess. You might not be the fastest or strongest—"

William held on to his objections.

"But you've helped maintain an even keel. Your decision-making and authority have kept us alive. You've remained level-headed and made mostly rational choices."

"Mostly?"

"Nobody's perfect. We owe you a lot. You're our protector."

Time to let his old dreams die. Edin belonged to a different life. A mum and dad he'd never see again. He'd taken on an extra responsibility whether he wanted it or not. He'd had to make decisions unlike any before. Decisions that affected those he cared about most.

Matilda stepped closer to William, pressing her body against his. They kissed, and he tasted the salt of her sweat. He inhaled through his nose, drinking in every second of the experience.

When they parted, William said, "I used to dream of that much more than I did of being a protector."

"Get down!"

Gracie's shriek sent ice through William's veins. "What?"

Her face red, her hands flapping with her words, Gracie said, "Get the fuck down. Now!"

A whining buzz in the distance. A thrumming hum, like the sound of a gigantic bee. It came from over their right shoulder, the stadium's roof blocking their line of sight.

"For the last time," Gracie yelled. "Get. Down."

Matilda dropped and pulled William with her. They crawled beneath the seats and watched the world through the gaps in the bleached blue plastic.

The hum grew louder. Three lights flew overhead with a *whoosh,* each of them dragging trails behind them like comets.

The buzz ran away from them, the giant metal insects shooting off into the distance. Matilda let out a hard exhale. "What the hell were they?"

"Who knows?" William said. "But I'm sure we'll find out."

CHAPTER 10

"I'm going to ask Gracie," William said.

But as he sat up, Matilda tugged him back down again. "Let her come over when it's safe. She knows this place better than us. There might be more of those ... *things*."

It made sense. "But what are they? Where do they come from? How are they flying? Are they alive?"

"Let her come to us. I'm sure she can answer your questions." Matilda held his hand, a slight tremble running through her. A stuttered burst came from the other side of the stadium, and she gripped harder. A series of metallic *tings*. A flash of white light. A roar. An orange glow of fire.

Gracie appeared over William and Matilda.

"What's going on?" William said.

Her attention divided between him and the commotion in the distance, Gracie said, "Drones."

"What?"

"Come on." Gracie reached a hand down and helped William to his feet. "Come with me."

They all ran through the seating area of the stadium. The closeness of the bleached blue chairs narrowed their paths.

The pyrotechnics continued in the sky over to their right. The stuttered bursts. The roar of flames.

They headed for a jagged hole in the stadium's far wall from where the sheet metal had been torn wide open, much like on the roof. Gracie leaped through and landed with a *clang* on the other side.

Where Olga had failed to trust Gracie before, she now leaped without missing a beat, mirroring Gracie's movements and landing on the other side of the hole with the slamming of her feet against metal.

William leaped last, Jezebel out in front of him so he didn't catch the axe on the sides of the gap. The metal platform belonged to a flight of zigzagged stairs, much like the ones on the other side that had led them to the stadium's roof. Gracie had already made it down three flights.

The white glow and bursting of orange flames appeared brighter now they were out of the stadium. The stuttered bursts, followed by the tings of spraying metal. The *whoosh* of erupting flames.

Gracie crossed a wider road than many they'd seen, leading them closer to the chaos. She ran around the back of a large square building and came to a halt on the far corner. She grabbed Olga before she could pass her and dragged her back.

When the others had gathered, Gracie held up the index finger on her right hand. "You get one look each. When you've looked, pull your head back in. The last thing we need is for them to see us."

Olga peered around the corner first. She pulled her head back almost instantly. The colour had drained from her face.

"Drones and robot dogs," Gracie explained while Max looked next.

"Although we don't get many soldiers out at night, those things are always on the streets. They're constantly at war."

Artan looked next and would have watched for longer had Gracie not pulled him back.

"So who are they fighting now?" Max said.

"Each other." Gracie pointed one way. "The drones belong to Fear." She pointed the other. "And the dogs belong to Fury."

"They seem to be quite an equal match," Hawk said. "The drones can fly away from the dogs' flames, and the dogs—"

"Are bulletproof," Gracie said.

William repeated it back to her. "Bulletproof?"

"The drones fire bullets. They'd tear through you or me, but the dogs have steel shells that the bullets can't penetrate. At least, not without the drones getting so close they'd get set on fire."

Finally, his turn to look, William leaned around the corner. The drones' bright white lights made his head spin as they zipped through the sky, weaving in and out of one another. Small discs about two feet in diameter and a foot thick, their torches looked like noses, and they had small arms hanging down beneath them. Red rings of heat lit up the ends of their little appendages as they sent a spray of metal at the dogs, who stood about a foot tall and two feet long. Built from black steel, they had glowing red eyes. Square heads, they had hinged jaws and belched fire. Even from this distance, the strength of their heat forced William to pull his head back.

"There's more technology here than you're used to," Gracie said.

William snorted a laugh. "You're telling me! So what's going to happen here? Who will win?"

Gracie peered around the corner. When she pulled back in, she shrugged. "I'd say neither. The environment doesn't favour either side. Sometimes the dogs catch the drones in a tight spot and keep them in range. Sometimes the drones get the jump on the dogs and get in so many shots they penetrate even the dogs' strong shells."

"So we shouldn't worry about what's happening out there?" Dianna said. "I mean, they're keeping each other busy, right?"

"Exactly," Gracie said. "It's only a problem if one of them sees you."

"Uh, Gracie."

Matilda's words sent a shiver through William. He knew her better than anyone. He knew exactly what that, *uh, Gracie* meant. Reluctant to turn around, yet he still followed Matilda's pointing finger. An alley across the way. Too tight for the moonlight to penetrate, it sat completely in shadow. Although, piercing the utter darkness was the glow of two red eyes.

"Shit," Gracie said. "Now we're screwed."

CHAPTER 11

A moment of stillness in a world of chaos. The battle between the drones and the dogs raged on around the corner, but it might as well have been in a different city. There were now more pressing matters at hand. Under the glaring scrutiny of those two red eyes, William reached for Matilda and touched the base of her back. He held the weight of Jezebel in his other hand.

The dog stepped from the alley with stilted movements. The orange and white glow from the fighting machines in the distance caught the edges of its scratched and dented body. Its red eyes glowed brighter for locking onto the enemy with a focus that wouldn't yield. The squeak of its mandible hinges ended in the *clack* of its jaw falling loose.

Gracie broke their collective inaction when she said, "Run!"

William took off after Gracie. Olga and Matilda were ahead of him, the others behind. The roar of flames, the heat at their backs.

They turned the bend and ran along the main road. The

dog's metal feet beat a tattoo against the hard asphalt. It gained on them despite its awkward gait.

"Hopefully," Artan said, "that's the only—"

The white glow from the drones' torches cut him off. They'd broken away from the battle with the dogs.

"As much as they will fight one another," Gracie said, "they'll take down a human target over a machine all day long. And they'll take down an enemy soldier over a civilian."

Another tower block on their left, Gracie darted into it, and Matilda followed.

Olga stopped at the door. She looked back at William and the others, but her attention fixed on Max. She slapped the base of her spear on the ground before tilting the pointy end into the building. "Why should we follow her? She was the one who led us into this mess."

The large foyer amplified Gracie's response. "Do what you want, Olga. I'm just trying to survive."

Much like the entrance to the tall towers, this block had rusting double doors at one end with a single doorway leading to a stairwell beside it. They must have been built from the same blueprint.

Gracie vanished into the stairwell, Matilda behind her. William paused halfway across the foyer and waited for the others. Dianna shot past him, then Hawk, Artan next, and Max, his war hammer gripped with both hands.

"Max!" Olga said. "What are you doing?"

"I'm following the only person who knows this city." His voice disappeared with him up the stairs, growing quieter as he got farther away. "If nothing else, she's trying to stay alive. I think we should follow her lead."

Olga remained outside. Then her eyes widened. She darted into the building, a stream of flames shooting across the block's entrance where she'd been only seconds before.

William charged into the stairwell, Olga a few feet behind.

The clack of the dog's strides entered the foyer. William called back to Olga, "I'm glad you decided to join us."

"Fuck you, William."

Were it not for the fiery death on their tails, William would have run anywhere but up another flight of stairs. His legs shook with fatigue, and he clamped his jaw as he battled the climb. Jezebel restricted his swinging arms, but he couldn't leave her. Not after everything they'd been through together.

Crash! Someone kicked open a steel door a few floors above.

The one-hundred-and-eighty-degree turns on the staircase made William's head spin like they had the last time. But with only two flights to the newly opened door, he pushed on, slamming into the concrete wall on his next turn, the stairwell so dark he had to rely on blind luck to find his footing.

William's friends gathered in the corridor. He let Olga past and kicked the steel door shut behind him with another *crash!* A thick bolt on the inside, he slid it home with a *clack!*

Olga called ahead to Gracie, "This is fucking suicide. And I will remind you of that."

"I'll look forward to the *I told you so* when I'm dead."

A thunder-crack of a slam hit the locked steel door. William spun around. Drone or dog, whichever one had hit it, they'd dented it on their first attack. Another *crack* bent it further. The glow of flames seeped through the gaps.

After the third slam, a square muzzle poked through a space beneath the door, the screeching of steel against steel as it tried to force its way in. The door cut a fresh silver groove into the top of its head. Bursts of flames shot from its snout. *Crack!* Another machine hit the door, bending it further. The inquisitive dog crawled through to its shoulders, its metal feet pawing at the concrete floor.

The others had already vanished around a bend in the corridor. William sprinted to catch up. Olga, at the back of his line of friends, ducked into a room ahead on her right.

If William hadn't witnessed it, there's no way he would have followed. But as he entered the room, Olga left it via a window. She stepped up onto the ledge and jumped for the building opposite, landing two-footed on a balcony about six feet away. All the while, she kept a hold of her spear.

The moonlight to guide him, a burst of fire behind, William muttered, "Don't look down!" Matilda in the hotel room opposite, he stepped onto the window and jumped, his arms windmilling as he crossed the gap. Several drones appeared on his right, blinding him in mid-air.

The stutter of bullets chewed into the brickwork of the tower he'd jumped from and pinged against the balcony he aimed for.

William's legs folded beneath him as he landed. Roaring agony slammed through his kneecaps when he hit the concrete floor. Jezebel skittered away.

Several pairs of hands dragged him to his feet and pulled him on. Max, Artan, and Matilda, Matilda holding on longer as she led him away.

The first of the dogs from the building opposite hit the wall above the balcony from where it had made the leap. Its heavy landing shook the floor. Several more of the creatures crashed down on top of it, the sprawling pile slowing all of their progress.

At the back of the line again, Gracie too far ahead to spot, William focused on Matilda directly in front of him. Another long hallway with a steel door at the end. The moonlight couldn't penetrate the darkness, but the drones obliged. Their dazzling white light peered through the windows into the building.

The hinges on the steel door groaned when Matilda knocked it wider. William shoulder-barged the metal barrier as he went through after her. But the door was lighter than he'd expected. It flew wide and cracked against the wall on the other side. William's momentum carried him over the first concrete stair leading down, and he fell sideways. He hit the stairs on his right side, giving him an instant dead arm, his legs sailing over his head.

Slamming into a concrete wall at the bottom of the first flight of stairs, William blinked in the windowless stairwell. He only had the steps of his friends to guide him. And they were heading up. "Shit!" His head throbbing, his body aching, his shins on fire, he patted the ground, found Jezebel, reached up for a handrail, and pulled himself to his feet.

The dim moonlight from an open door a floor or two higher up, William climbed the flight of stairs he'd fallen down, acrid smoke in the air from where the dogs' flames burned anything in their path. He made it up another flight in time for the first of the dogs to appear. They barrelled through the door like he had, tripped on the stairs, and fell down the first flight. At least he wasn't the only one.

The others had again slowed their pace to allow William to catch up. They waited in a corridor a few floors above, Gracie at the front, Matilda closest to him. Were there time for rest, they probably would have given it to him, but the second he appeared, Gracie nodded and took off again.

Gracie vanished into a room on her left, and instead of jumping for the building opposite, she dropped her spear, leaving it behind as she hung from the balcony, shimmied down so her legs were close to her destination, swung towards the building, and dropped, landing two-footed on the balcony below.

At the back of the line again, William waited in the room while the others followed Gracie's path, all of them discarding their larger weapons.

The dogs' clattering ascent in the stairwell spoke of their difficulty with the climb. Hopefully, it would give William and the others the time they needed. And it might have, had the blinding light from the drones not appeared outside. Red rings on the ends of their small arms, they sprayed the building with bullets.

Max, Olga, and Matilda ahead of him, Max jumped back into the room, took shelter behind a wall, and threw his arms wide. "What do we do?"

Matilda picked up what must have once been a table. Now only a frame, the glass was absent from the tabletop, as it had been from most other things in this city. "Move aside." She launched the frame from the balcony. It drew the drones' bullets, giving her time to swing over the railing, slide down, and then drop to the balcony below. She'd given them the blueprint to follow.

Olga launched an old chair for Max to go next, and then another one for herself. Max had left his war hammer, Olga her spear.

"Fuck it!" William launched Jezebel. She spun through the air as the first of the dogs charged into the room. The stutter of bullets followed his projectile while he swung around the balcony, slid down the railings so fast the rust-coated metal burned his palms, and dropped to the balcony on the floor below.

The first of the dogs caught up and leaped for the building opposite. It let out a continuous stream of fire as it spun through the air. The flames caught a drone and sent it into a spin that ended with an explosion against a wall to William's left. The other dogs halted on the balcony above. They spewed flames, but were unable to angle them down.

William, lighter and more mobile without his weapon, chased after the others.

CHAPTER 12

The dogs weren't stupid. Where one of them had jumped and fallen, the others halted and turned around. They'd find another way, and they were fast enough to catch up. William reached the stairwell at the same time as the creatures on the floor above. Were it not for their searing ball of flames, he might have fallen again. But they lit his way, even if he ran with the reek of his own singed hair in his nostrils.

Like the dogs before it, the first of the creatures tripped on the stairs. The stairwell shook from where its heavy steel body stumbled and slammed to an abrupt halt against the wall at the end of the first flight.

Matilda held a door open for William two floors down, the number one just visible on the wall beside her.

Gracie led them along another corridor similar to the others. She took them to yet another room. No balcony this time, but the drop from the window was no more than fifteen feet.

Matilda jumped, and as William leaped from the window,

the crash of the steel door leading to the stairwell broke open. The *clack-clack* of the dogs' uneven gait swarmed in.

William landed on the hard and unforgiving road with a jolt. Had Gracie not led them, he wouldn't have chosen this route. But thank the heavens they had because a swarm of drones waited for them on the ground floor. They lit up the inside of the derelict building, the focus of their lights on the doorway exiting the stairwell as they waited for William and his friends.

They were through their second abandoned shop when the crash of a dog slammed down on the road behind them. A *whoosh* of flames, for what good it did. They were too far back for it to have any effect.

Another wide road separated them from another cluster of towers. The buildings were so close together, they were damn near touching. Even closer than the ones they'd leaped between earlier.

The first of the dogs appeared as William entered the next tower. Its awkward bounding gait, its square head, its glowing red eyes. These things didn't tire, and they wouldn't quit. So much for the lead they'd gained.

Gracie took them into another stairwell, the snaking concrete stairs like many of the others. William's legs burned with the effort of the climb. At some point his body would fail him. Until then, he'd have to keep going. Either that or die.

Gracie's breathless voice echoed in the dark. "First, we lose the dogs, and then we lose the drones."

At least she had a plan. She'd done this before, right?

Too dark to see the numbers on the wall, if this building even labelled their floors, so William counted instead. Past the door to the third floor, Gracie three to four floors above him and still climbing.

William reached the sixth floor when Gracie kicked a door open several floors above.

He stumbled into the corridor on the tenth floor. Stairs would only give them an advantage over the dogs as long as he could climb them. Stars swam in his vision, every deep inhale failing to sate his need for air.

Matilda jumped through the window at the end of the hallway, the *tock* of her feet landing on the metal walkway outside.

More stairs. Like the ones running up the side of the stadium. They clung to the tower and mirrored the internal stairwell in their zigzagging path up or down. They went up. Of course they went up!

Rust had claimed several steps, much like the ones outside the arena. It left a gap of about six feet in the next flight of stairs. Six feet wide and three feet higher up. Horizontal bars ran beneath the stairs directly above them. Matilda copied Gracie, Max, Artan, and Olga. She leaped, caught the bar, and swung across the gap, landing two-footed on the other side. But Dianna had halted, Hawk beside her. "Go! Now!" William screamed as he charged at the girl. "The dogs are coming."

Dianna screamed, jumped for the horizontal bar, caught it and swung across.

As she let go of the bar, William leaped. Hawk ran back towards the dogs.

William landed on the other side, his stomach lurching as he teetered on the edge of his balance before Max and Artan pulled him towards them. The fall through the gap might have only been ten feet, but it would have been a ten-foot drop onto metal stairs. He'd been lucky so far. No chance he would have managed this fall without breaking something.

Hawk waited by the window they'd escaped from. The first dog jumped out onto the walkway. He caught it and flipped the thing over the railing, his muscles bulging as he launched it away from the stairs. Like the one earlier, it breathed fire as it spun, slamming against the ground over one hundred feet below. Its body lay broken on the asphalt.

The next dog through the window emerged at such a speed it slammed into the railing on the walkway and bent the steel bar. Hawk had already climbed back up the stairs. As he leaped the six-foot gap, the creature breathed fire and leaped after him.

William helped Max catch Hawk, and all three of them dropped into a hunch, the dog's fire shooting over their heads. But the gap proved too much, and the creature fell, immobilised by its heavy landing.

Dog after dog attempted the jump. Every one of them came up short, falling with the others, an ever-growing pile on the stairs below. Many of them survived the fall, but not a single one attempted to climb the stairs again.

"How did you know you'd be safe?" William said.

Hawk shook his head. "I didn't. But from how they climbed the stairs, I assumed they'd struggle with the jump."

William nodded down at their retreat. "It looks like they know it too."

"We're not out of this yet," Gracie said. "The dogs might be down, but we still have to think about the drones."

CHAPTER 13

They might have been far from the ground on the tower's roof, but at least they could see where they were heading. The moon shone as if it lit the way specifically for them. Exhausted, battered, and bruised, William ran with heavy steps, his mouth wide as he gasped for air.

The gaps between the buildings only stretched a few feet. Easy enough when they weren't twenty stories up. Every jump sent a flip through William's stomach. He focused ahead. Don't look down!

They were several buildings away from the one they'd lost the dogs on. Every roof had a doorway leading back inside. Gracie chose this one to re-enter the dark stairwell.

As he had before, William took up the rear, Matilda directly in front. The hum of a drone froze him to the spot. The machine's brilliant white torch pinned him where he stood. "Shit!"

The drone's guns whirred. Red rings of heat. Bullets burst towards him.

Matilda grabbed William's shirt and dragged him inside.

The bullets hit the closing steel door. "What were you doing?" she said.

William's words had left him. He shook his head. "I … I …" He should have run the second he'd heard them.

"Come on!" Matilda dragged him down the stairs with her, the stampede of the others at least three to four floors below. "We have drones on our tail," she called.

Gracie's reply snapped over the staccato beat of their descent. "Fuck it!"

The drones weren't stupid. They'd find them. But with no windows in the stairwell, maybe they could still get away.

The open door let in enough light to reveal the floor number. They were down to the tenth floor when Gracie made her move. Like she'd done with the other buildings, she turned into a room with a balcony that faced an opposing tower. The one they'd only just crossed the roof of. Were it not for her leadership, they'd all be dead by now.

William leaped last. An easy jump, his arms windmilled during his moment of weightlessness. The glow from a drone shone down on him. Splinters of brickwork sprayed from where the bullets chewed into the wall.

Gracie led them to another stairwell. She took them down several more floors before they jumped across to another building.

This time, William, as the last runner, got clear with no sign of the drones.

A sparse layout of windows lit the next stairwell. Gracie led them past the ground floor to the end of the stairs in the basement. She charged through the final steel door. The others followed, but before William could run after them, Matilda subtly raised her hand in his direction. He knew her well enough to read her intention. Stay the fuck back!

The door closed on William, but not before he saw why

she'd encouraged him to wait. Twenty to thirty boys, girls, men, and women in red uniforms sat around a fire in an underground space, ramps leading out of there. One of the men got to his feet. Thankfully, he only carried a baton. They could fight batons. But could they fight twenty to thirty of them?

William had to do something. He ran, retreating up the stairs. As he rounded the first bend back to the ground floor, a deep male voice echoed in the cavernous space. The man addressed his friends. "Well, well, what have we here, then?"

CHAPTER 14

William's legs burned, sweat stung his eyes, and his lungs were so tight he had permanent stars swimming in his vision. But he climbed the stairs to the ground floor and out into the foyer.

His steps heavy, his feet slapping against the tiled floor, William stumbled towards the road outside and waited in the open. They'd taken so many twists and turns he'd lost his bearings. Had they gotten clear of the area filled with mines? He'd have to take his chances. The hum of the drones in the distance told him everything he needed to know. The swarm was on its way.

First, the low thrum of their engines, and then their bright white glow. As the whir grew louder and the lights shone brighter, William jogged along the front of the tower, watching over his shoulder for the drones.

And he'd timed it to perfection. The drones rounded the corner and fixed on him just as he turned and sprinted away. The collective buzz of the flying machines came after him. They flew in a V formation. At least fifteen to twenty of them, they had him in their sights.

By the time William had rounded the next bend, they'd halved his lead and were closing in fast. Another spray of bullets ate into a wall close to him.

His steps clumsy, his stomach knotted. The bullets chewed into the asphalt just feet behind him. William charged around the next corner. A slope led to the space beneath the tower. A ramp of some sort. He let gravity carry him down.

As one, the soldiers in red turned towards William, his own breathing the loudest thing in that moment.

The man who'd approached his friends threw his arms wide. He had black bags beneath his blue eyes and scars on his cheeks. He shook his head. "What the hell is—"

The angry swarm of drones flooded into the basement behind William.

A girl in their group stated the obvious. "Drones!"

William ran past his friends and shouted, "Follow me!"

He led them back through the steel door, the crash of the slamming metal as it flew wide into the wall. Up the first flight of stairs, they ran to the foyer and out into the moonlit street beyond. The stutter of bullets echoed in the building's basement. The screams of dying soldiers rang even louder.

Although they continued to run away from the tower, they slowed their pace. The dogs would take a while to regroup, and the drones were occupied. They moved slowly enough for William to catch his breath. "You said the drones would go for Fury over anyone else."

Gracie smiled and patted him on the back. "That I did. Well done, William. Well done."

CHAPTER 15

The longest night William had endured in a long time. Maybe the longest night ever. And they were still hours from sunrise. He ran with the others on legs that had no right carrying his weight. Every time his tired steps slammed down on the concrete, sharp bruising pain ran up the front of his shins. He'd whacked them when he'd fallen on the stairs, but the general abuse he'd subjected his body to had left him aching from head to toe.

William ran at the back of the line again, Matilda and then Olga ahead of him. Max hadn't been his usual self since Cyrus' death, and this run through the city hadn't helped. He did what the group needed of him, but his expression had remained unchanged the entire time. Blank. Distant. Dianna had kept up without complaint. Artan could run forever, as could Hawk, who would also fight anything in his path given half the chance. Olga refused to back down to Gracie's pressure, and Matilda rarely came up short when tested. She conducted herself with humility, but she was the strongest person William had ever met.

Gracie darted through another open and windowless

space into another building, shards of glass popping beneath their steps. This one had machines like the café they'd visited when they'd entered the city. Attached to the walls, they were missing their fronts, their sun-bleached multicoloured wires spilling from them like intestines.

A staircase in the corner, Gracie headed for it.

"Not again," William said beneath his breath. "More fucking stairs."

All the while, the pulse of gunfire rang throughout the city as the drones executed the soldiers. But screw them. Who knew what they'd planned to do with William's friends. They deserved everything that came their way.

The upstairs of the abandoned shop had one small window. Like all the others in the city, the glass had gone from the frame. Like some less trodden paths, shards of it remained, the fine dust glistening like glitter in the moonlight.

Gracie peered out of the small window while William slumped against a wall. If he stayed still for too long, he'd seize. His body buzzed from where sweat burned his many grazes. He reached across and held Matilda's hand, resting the back of his head against the wall. Just as he closed his eyes, Gracie spoke.

"Those marks on your map, William."

The lure of sleep had already wrapped its arms around him. William snapped out of it, snorting with a sharp inhalation. "Huh?"

"Those marks on your map." Gracie held her hand out to him.

William pulled the map from his back pocket before handing it to Gracie. She unfolded it on the floor. "These marks." According to the map, they were between two communities of similar size. Both of them had orange boxes. The communities that were farther south had boxes that were a deeper shade of red. "They show how technologically advanced each place is."

"How do you know that?" Artan said.

"This map comes from our community. It's one reason we're not on here. We create maps to throw people off the scent. Although," she smirked, "I'm fairly confident that if anyone else made a map of the area, they still wouldn't include us. We're one of the best-kept secrets around these parts."

"Based on whose opinion?" Olga said.

Matilda spoke before Gracie could reply. "So Fear and Fury are only orange?"

Gracie shrugged.

The white glow of a drone's light shot past the window. Artan pointed at where it had just gone. "Drones and dogs only warrant an orange box?"

Again, Gracie shrugged.

Max's eyes remained glazed when he said, "What does a community with a red box look like?"

Footsteps entered the ground floor of the building.

Gracie jogged on tiptoes to the top of the stairs. Hawk closed in behind her and drew his hunting knife. William reached them last, his movements stiff.

Two soldiers dressed in blue. Fear's army. They'd entered the building from the opposite end to the group. They were clearly heading for their drones. Had they been following their flying machines the entire time? A shot of adrenaline tightened William's stomach. Had they been on his tail when he'd lured the drones into the basement of the tall building?

"Come on, man," one soldier said to the other. Two boys of a similar age to William and his friends. The one who'd spoken had his hand on his comrade's back. "We need to join the others."

"I need a piss. You go and I'll catch you up."

"Fine." The other soldier ran out into the street.

The remaining soldier heaved, his entire body snapping forward at the waist. His bark echoed through the room and ended with a splash of sick hitting the hard floor.

William turned away and pressed the back of his hand to his nose. He couldn't blame the boy for his nerves, but he didn't need to smell it.

Gracie spoke in a gentle whisper. "He's probably a rookie. No doubt this is his first taste of battle. He's probably shitting himself. Not that I blame him. Life as a soldier in this city ain't easy. Especially when you're dragged into a fight, and especially when you belong to Fear's army."

"What's the difference?" Dianna said.

"From what we understand, Fury's citizens choose if they want to fight in their army. The citizens of Fear have no such luxury. If you're old enough, or sometimes you only have to be large enough, they dress you in a blue uniform, put a baton in your hand, and send you to war with a hearty slap on the back."

The boy downstairs heaved again.

"Hawk!" Olga lunged for the stocky hunter. She missed, grabbing air where he'd been seconds before.

Hawk slipped down the stairs.

The soldier's next heave got cut short, Hawk gripping him in a headlock.

Gracie's face twisted, her skin puce. "What's he doing?"

"Am I his fucking minder?" Olga said.

A scuffle played out, and a few seconds later, Hawk emerged, the muscles in his right arm bulging from where he dragged the soldier up the stairs.

Even Max's expression had changed, his jaw hanging loose.

Hawk dragged the soldier into the middle of the room and dropped him on the floor.

When the blue uniformed boy opened his mouth to scream, Gracie shoved Hawk aside and kicked the kid in the head. The *crack* of her connection whipped around the room. Fear's soldier fell limp.

Gracie bared her teeth at the still-grinning Hawk. Veins stood out on her neck, and her eyes bulged. "What are you doing?"

Hawk's grin fell. He looked at the others. While they might not have levelled the same rage on him, from the way his expression sagged further, he realised he'd done something wrong. He pointed at the soldier. "I thought I'd eliminate the threat."

"What threat?" Gracie hands slapped against her thighs from where she'd thrown up a hard shrug. "He was puking his guts up. All you've done is blown our cover."

"But I-I—"

"You what, Hawk? Is there really a sane justification for what you've just done?"

"I wanted to protect everyone."

"But you've done the exact opposite." The ginger girl tapped her temple. "If you used that small brain of yours and *thought* for a second …" Her cheeks bulged with her exhale. "We were in hiding up here. We could have rested and waited for this to pass."

Just the mention of rest dragged on William's frame.

"B—"

"What do we do now when someone comes looking for him? Because they will."

"I thought a hostage would come in handy."

"We're trying to get out of this city. What do we want a hostage for? We want nothing from them."

Artan stepped between the two. "It's done now. The question is, what the hell do we do with him?"

"Jason?"

The soldier's partner had returned to the shop. Gracie shook her head at Hawk while pulling her knife from the back of her belt.

William reached the top of the stairs by the time Gracie stepped from the bottom. The blue soldier turned her way, his mouth hanging open, his response silenced by the hard *crack* of Gracie's knife entering the top of his skull.

They joined Gracie downstairs. She levelled her blood-soaked blade on Hawk. "Next time, use your fucking brain, yeah?"

"I just—"

"You screwed up, Hawk," Matilda said. "Accept it and shut up."

Hawk frowned and stumbled back as if Matilda's chastisement had a physicality to it.

"Now maybe we can still get out of here." Gracie lifted the dead soldier, hooking a hand under each armpit. Olga helped, the two girls heading towards the stairs. "If we can get this soldier upstairs, at least it'll take them a while to find him. It might give us the time we need."

The room lit up with a bright white glow. A drone fixed on them. Its guns whirred.

"Shit!" Gracie dropped the corpse. "Follow me!" She ran through the back of the shop.

Adrenaline came to William's aid again. Driven by a hard surge, he followed his friends out of the derelict building.

CHAPTER 16

The glow from the drone's brilliant white beam sent the group's shadows streaking ahead of them, stretched-out versions of their fleeing selves. At least it drove away William's fatigue. He could push through that, but maybe not the numb buzz in his shins. How long before that pain got the better of him? At some point it would hit him with both barrels, and he'd grind to a halt. Hopefully, that moment would come after they'd found safety.

Gracie set a demanding pace with her zigzagging run. An example of how to avoid being shot.

At the rear again, Matilda directly ahead of him, William ran left and then right, all the while trying to keep up with the rest. Each sudden change in direction could be his last, his legs wobbling, threatening to give. The sharp chips of asphalt spurred him on. They sprayed a stinging attack against his calves and the backs of his thighs from where the drone tried and failed to execute him.

Gracie led them left down a tight alley.

Seconds after William entered, the place glowed with the drone's bright white glare, but the sharp turn made it crash into one wall and then the other. The battle for control halted its fire.

William reached the end and turned left. Another main road, but at least the alley had slowed the drone. Gracie led them into another shop like she had the route mapped out in her mind.

William ducked the spray of plaster from the wall on his left. The drone too far away to hit them. It clearly realised the same. The bullets stopped again. Why waste ammo? It had to run out at some point, right?

Matilda called back to him, "You okay?"

His lungs were tighter than ever. His response would rob him of the breaths he needed. The gap grew between him and Matilda. He waved her on when she turned to look at him. "Just keep running!"

The high street behind them, Gracie ran for another gigantic building. Its entrance made from a steel frame, the remains of the windows it would have once held lay spread out in a glistening mess on the ground. Fifty feet wide and as tall, this place must have shone like a jewel in its day.

The floor was made from dirty white tiles, each one a foot square. Many were cracked, and many more were missing.

"Why have we come in here?" Artan shouted.

Gracie pushed on. A conversation would slow them down.

The drone shot through a gap in the steel frame, entering the building behind them.

Gracie turned right into what looked like another shop. They'd entered an indoor high street. They followed her, a few of the drone's bullets shattering the ceramic tiles.

Old racks with pegs. Another clothes shop! William had only seen a small part of this city, but he'd already passed through enough clothes shops to serve this community ten times over.

The drone's whining buzz of its propellors. The slap of their steps hit the hard ceramic tiles.

The metal frames forced them in a weaving run. It helped them avoid the intermittent bullet fire. William took a sharp left, stumbled where his right leg buckled, and slammed into another rack, knocking the eight-foot frame so hard it crashed to the ground.

The drone attacked it.

Another sharp turn and William stumbled again. It slowed him down, so he kicked over another metal rack. The loud *crash* drew the drone's fire.

A narrow doorway at the back of the store, Gracie vanished into it, Olga next. Dianna, Max, Hawk, and Artan followed. Matilda slowed, but William yelled, "Get in there now!" She followed the others.

William kicked over one more frame. The drone zeroed in on it while he ran through the narrow doorway and jumped aside, covering his face from the spray of debris kicked up by the drone's next attack.

Gracie had already made it up several flights of stairs, and she kept climbing. But William waited. He leaned against the hard and cold wall and dragged air into his lungs, avoiding the drone's sensor when the white light of its torch shone into the stairwell. Did it know he was there? Would it wait for him? They weren't built to manage enclosed spaces like stairwells.

As if answering his question, the light dulled from where it turned around and flew away. Surely it would try to meet them higher up.

The gap running through the middle of the stairs showed William that Gracie had chosen her floor. A hole in the roof let moonlight into the gloomy space. Olga had gone from sight also, Dianna vanishing through the doorway next.

But Matilda had stopped. She waited just one floor above. It didn't matter how much he wanted to rest, they couldn't afford to get separated out here. He couldn't be the reason she lost track of the group.

The first flight of stairs consisted of only twelve steps. William misjudged the height of the final one, caught his toe, and stumbled forwards. He hit the ground with both knees, clenching his jaw as spasms crawled up the insides of his thighs into his groin.

"William?" The patter of Matilda's steps came down to him. "Are you okay?"

His mouth stretched wide, every shred of his being focused on catching his breath. His body throbbed; his shins and knees burned. "I can't … keep going. I can't do it. I need to stop. I really hurt myself when I fell down those stairs in one of the towers. You go without me. I'll meet you at … the metal tower." Stars swam in his vision, and were his stomach not empty, he would have vomited.

Matilda shook her head and helped him to his feet. "You need to get up now. I won't give up on you." Instead of leading him upstairs, she led him back down again.

"Where are we going?" William pointed up. "We need to get moving so we can keep on their tail."

Matilda shook her head. "We can't catch them now."

Sweat burned William's eyes. He blinked repeatedly, for what good it did. Now the drone had gone, they only had the light of the moon to guide them. He could just make out where the light touched the tips of Matilda's features. The end of her nose. The glisten of her brown eyes.

"What are we going to—"

"Shh!" Matilda pressed her finger to her lips.

The burst of bullets called to them from the other side of

the building. The drone must have found Gracie and the others.

"Now!" Matilda tugged on William's hand, leading him at a fast walk back out into the shop they'd just exited.

His steps clumsy, but at least they moved at a more manageable pace.

Matilda halted again at the shop's exit before she peered out, looking both left and right. "Come on," she said, "let's go."

The distant fire of bullets echoed through the dead city. Hopefully, all their friends would be there when they reached the metal tower.

Matilda led William across a small car park, away from the large building filled with shops. They entered another tower block.

They climbed the concrete stairs to the first floor. Many more stretched up away from them, but this level seemed as good as any. They found an empty apartment. The silver moonlight shone through the window. A smaller space than the rooms in the hotels, but palatial compared to anything in Edin.

Still fighting to recover his breath, the sound of conflict rode on the breeze soaring through the city. It came from the direction of the tower where the drones had ambushed the soldiers. They had no chance against that many indefatigable drones. Even if it took all night, there would only be one winner.

"I would have stayed with them had I been able to," William said.

Matilda nodded before reaching out to hold his hands. She sat down, encouraging him to do the same with a gentle tug. "I know. We need to make our own way now. But first, we need to rest. I think we're safe here for the time being."

CHAPTER 17

Olga matched Gracie step for step. She might have the others convinced, but Olga wouldn't fall for her charm. Someone had to remain vigilant, and that bitch had too many secrets. If shit got real, she'd leave them in a heartbeat. She talked about taking the group to her community. Someone needed to make sure she delivered on that promise.

Gracie slowed at the top of the stairs.

A line of windows along one side of the vast room let in the moonlight. Clothes rails in one section, much like Olga had seen in several other shops. But in another section, there were steel frames from old tables, chairs, and beds. Then in another corner of the huge room sat a line of off-white plastic boxes with windows on the front. The glass remained in most of them, albeit with a spider-webbing of cracks. Those that had lost their screens were filled with wires like some of the other dead machines in this city. "What is this place?" Olga said.

"It used to be a department store."

"A what?"

"A massive shop that sold everything you could want, from clothes to furniture to electronics."

Olga's eyes stung with her sweat. She wiped them with her dirty sleeve. "Why didn't people just make what they wanted?"

"It was easier not to."

"Huh?"

A second to catch her breath, Gracie gulped with a dry *click.*

Olga swallowed against the same parched itch, her saliva a paste in her arid mouth.

"There was a time," Gracie said, "when people travelled from one side of this world to the other. They'd gotten so good at it, it worked out cheaper and easier to get someone in a faraway country to make something for you and bring it over."

"What? That's impossible."

"I think—" Gracie leaned forwards and rested her hands on her knees "—the word you're looking for is unsustainable."

"Don't tell me what words I'm looking for."

Gracie raised an eyebrow. "Well, it was."

Max, Artan, Dianna, and Hawk all joined them one at a time, bursting from the top of the stairs. Gracie leaned to one side, looking past them. "Where are Matilda and William?"

Olga ran back and peered down into the darkness. She turned her palms to the sky and shook her head. "They've gone."

"What the hell?" Gracie said. "Is it that hard to listen to what I say?"

"Maybe they had a better plan," Olga said.

"And what plan's that? To get themselves killed?"

Olga balled her fists. "We're not wet behind the ears, you know? We've been through enough shit to help us make good choices. If they've gone a different way, it's for a good reason. Maybe they don't trust you."

"Really? After all I've done."

"After all you've done?" Olga stepped towards Gracie only to meet Max's restraining arm.

Gracie shook her head. "So what do we do now?"

"We wait," Artan said. "They'll be here. We just need—"

A white searchlight glare cut across the abandoned store. The deep hum of a drone's propellers. The flying disc shot through one of the window frames on the far side, tearing across the decaying junk.

"I'm going," Gracie said. "It's your choice if you come with me or not."

While the girl who'd led them this far weaved through the rails and remnants of a long-forgotten life, Olga, Artan, Max, Hawk, and Dianna waited.

"Look, Artan," Olga said. "We're in this together, and we stand by you." The drone's thrumming buzz grew louder. "But what good are we to the others if we're dead?"

As if backing up Olga's argument, the whir of the drone's guns spun. The ends lit up as red rings before the stuttered burst of bullet fire spewed forth. They all ducked. The bullets played percussion on their environment.

If they waited any longer, they'd lose sight of Gracie. "Come on." Olga tugged Artan's hand. The first step kick-started him into action. They ran after Gracie, Olga at the front.

The drone's light showed them the way. They had a fifty-foot lead on the machine. Gracie about another fifty feet ahead of them. Then she vanished.

"What the fuck?" Hawk said.

The drone gained on the group. The *ting* of bullets hit the surrounding metal. But it fired less than before. It must have been running out of ammo. If only they knew how much it had left.

Gracie had dropped through a hole in the floor. Just about wide enough for a person. The drone wouldn't be able to follow.

Olga dropped to her front and slid backwards. Gracie caught her and helped her land.

The rest went through one at a time. Artan slid through last, pausing for one last check.

"Still no sign of them?" Olga said.

A shake of his head, Artan moved aside while holding his arms above him as protection. Chips of floor tile sprayed down on them. Red-hot streaks from where the bullets flew over the hole. The drone got closer. Its attack chewed into the floor where they'd stood, but it couldn't get an angle on them.

Stairs at the opposite end of the building like the ones they'd climbed to avoid the drone originally, Gracie reached them first and shoulder-barged through the steel door. This time, she led them down.

Small windows let in some light, but not enough. Olga ran on faith, following the sound of Gracie's steps, wincing every time her foot landed in case it twisted beneath her.

They'd climbed four floors to get to the shop above, but they now went down five. No windows on the final two floors, they ran blind. A metal rail on her right, pockmarked with rust, Olga held onto it for guidance, the friction like sandpaper against her palm. A white flash slammed through her vision when she collided with Gracie nose-first. Her eyes watered and her sinuses burned. She shoved the girl in front of her. "You could have fucking told me you'd stopped."

As Olga said it, Artan slammed into her back, sending all three of them sprawling.

Hawk fell over them next before Olga finally called,

"Max! Dianna! Slow down! We've stopped at the bottom of the stairs."

When they were all back on their feet, and Max and Dianna had joined them, Gracie said, "Follow me."

The creak of old hinges helped Olga pinpoint the door's location. She reached out, the steel barrier cold and rough with corrosion. Metal doors were the only ones that had lasted in this place.

A long, straight, and tight tunnel. The glow of moonlight about two hundred feet away showed them their destination. A thick pipe up to their right ran the entire length. It dominated the space, forcing Olga to walk with her head cocked to the left.

Their tired steps scraped the concrete floor. They all gasped for breath. Gracie spoke in between lungfuls. "When we get to the end of this tunnel, we should have bought ourselves some time. Even the drone will struggle to find us."

∾

OLGA HAD CAUGHT her breath by the time she got close to the end of the tunnel. Max walked directly behind her. She turned to him. "What an evening, eh?"

Max cleared his throat.

"Are you okay?"

"Yeah, I'm fine."

"I can't help you if you don't let me in."

"Thank you, Olga, but I'm not asking you to help me. Let's chat later when we don't have to be quiet, yeah?"

The moonlight stung Olga's eyes when she stepped from the dark tunnel. The pipe they'd travelled with took a nosedive through the ground. "What did they use that pipe for?"

"Sewage," Gracie said.

"What now?"

"Waste. Human waste."

"Ew. They had that much of it?"

"Look at this place, Olga. In its day, it pulled in thousands of people a week."

"That's a lot of shit," Hawk said.

Gracie laughed. "It's a lot of buckets to carry if you don't think of smarter ways to dispose of it. Not all the old ways were illogical. Some of them we've—"

The low growl of a nearby diseased halted Gracie. They were in a small car park. Surrounded by buildings and alleyways. Surrounded by darkness.

"It's that way!" Hawk—hunched and ready for war—pointed with the tip of his knife.

"So we run—" Gracie's sentence got cut short again. She'd been hooking a thumb away from them in the opposite direction to the sound, but Hawk had already charged.

Artan turned to Olga with wide eyes. "What shall I do?" But he didn't give her time to answer. She might have suggested they leave Hawk if he had. "I have to go after him."

As Hawk and then Artan vanished into the shadows, the screams of the diseased creature grew louder. Gracie bounced on her toes, her long plait flicking one way and then the other with her sharp head movements. "That noise isn't good. They'll bring more diseased to us."

"You're not suggesting we run, are you?"

"I'm not suggesting *you* do anything, Olga. I, however, am going to keep moving. Hawk's a liability. I refuse to die because of his stupidity." Gracie pointed at the large metal tower she'd set as their destination, now much closer than when she'd first shown it to them. "They know where to meet us."

More screams joined the fight.

At first, Gracie moved away from the battle with slow steps. Olga and the others could follow her if they wished.

"What shall we do?" Dianna chewed on her bottom lip, her attention divided between Gracie and where Artan and Hawk had gone.

Olga pointed after Gracie. "I don't trust her. I feel like I need to keep an eye on her."

Diseased screams came from another part of their dark surroundings. Dianna said, "Gracie was right. They're going to bring more of them to us. I worry I'll be more of a hindrance in a fight against the diseased. I'm not cut out for it."

"You go after Gracie," Max said, shoving the girl away from them. And then to Olga, he said, "Artan and Hawk might need my help. We'll meet you at the tower. Wait for us, okay?"

Before Max ran off, Olga grabbed both of his hands. She pulled him close. Their noses touched, their lips hovering an inch from the kiss she so longed for. "Be careful, okay?"

Max's tormented glaze cleared. Olga's entire being buzzed. He hadn't looked at her in that way in weeks. She kissed his stubbled cheek. "We'll be waiting for you."

Max smiled. "You'd best be."

"Come on." Dianna tugged on Olga's arm. More diseased screamed from yet another part of the city. "We need to go now."

Olga nodded several times as the shadows claimed Max. She would see him again. He'd be fine. He survived, that's what he did. She ran after Dianna, who chased after Gracie.

CHAPTER 18

The night sky had turned from black to dark blue with the start of a new day. Damp hung in the air and clung to Olga's clothes. Hard to tell where her sweat ended and the dew began. Every step clumsy, she fell forwards with her run, Dianna ahead of her, Gracie in the lead.

They passed through the tight alleyways of what Gracie had called the city's residential district. A residential district minus the residents. They'd left the large tower blocks and stadiums behind. They were now surrounded by houses. Who knew what stared from every paneless window or shadowy doorway? But they could only deal with what stood in their way. They couldn't go to war with what they couldn't see.

From a distance, the metal tower stood as a tall skeletal frame. Almost as if it had been abandoned mid-construction. But when Olga broke free from the final alley amongst the dense press of buildings, she finally saw the bottom section of the sixty-foot structure. Four legs spread out wide, one in each corner of its square base. Steel panels between the legs turned the space beneath into a room of sorts. A shelter. A storage area. A prison … She slowed her pace.

The side facing them had a dirty steel door. Like most metal in the city, it wore a rash of orange rust. For all intents and purposes, the tower stood as yet another dead artefact in a city filled with dead artefacts.

Gracie reached the door, checked left and right over each shoulder, and opened it. The hinges offered a cackling protest. She ushered in Dianna and then Olga before entering herself and closing the door, throwing them into complete darkness.

Gracie's voice echoed, bouncing off the hard walls. "At some point very soon—" she caught her breath "—I need to be heading back to my community. And I need to do it before daylight."

"That doesn't give us long," Olga said.

"No."

"Why can't you wait a little longer?"

"Two reasons. One, this city is much busier in the daytime, so our chances of avoiding capture are seriously reduced."

"And the second?" Dianna said.

"My community is well hidden. Even if we don't get captured, I can't risk exposing one of its entrances. Our strength lies in our camouflage. If either Fear or Fury find us, we'll be overrun."

"So you're going to abandon us like I said you would?"

"How am I abandoning you? I've done everything within my power to lead you lot to my community. For some reason, William and Matilda decided they knew a better way. And Hawk wants to fight anything he can. They're the ones who have screwed this up, not me."

Olga balled her hands into fists. "Don't you think there's a reason why they stopped? Maybe they needed our help. But we just carried on, didn't we?"

"And Hawk," Gracie said, "are you saying he had a better reason? To me, it looked like he wanted to continue his one-man crusade to defeat every enemy on the planet. I won't risk my life because of their mistakes. I told you I'd lead you here. I've done that. I can take Dianna back with me. Why don't you come with us, too?"

"Have you and Dianna already decided she's going with you?"

"I just assumed ..." Gracie said.

Dianna cleared her throat. Her voice came out as a weak warble. Were it not pitch black, Olga might have swung for the pathetic bitch. "What use am I to you here? I can't fight."

Company. She'd give Olga company. But how could she say that? A free and independent spirit, could she really admit she needed a friend to stay with her? To hold her hand in the darkness.

"Come with us," Dianna said.

"What about the others?"

A small red light blinked in the corner of the room.

"What's that?" Olga said.

"A camera. It's hooked up to my community."

"What's a camera?"

"It's a way for us to see who's waiting here. It's some of the new technology I said you'd see."

"Like the dogs and drones?"

"Sure," Gracie said, "but it can't harm you. It just helps us see if there's someone who needs rescuing. Like when Hawk and the others finally get here. Or Matilda and William."

"But it's dark."

"It sees in the dark."

"And what if they need our help before they get this far? What then?"

"I've done enough, Olga. I'll come and get them if they arrive, but they're on their own now."

Olga's shoulders slumped. "You do what you need to do. I can't leave this city without my friends. And, Dianna, you need to do what you think's right."

"It's not what I think's right," Dianna said. "It's what I think is best. I truly believe I will be a hindrance to you if I stay."

"Right, best, whatever ... If you think it's *best* to go to Gracie's community with her after all we've done for you, then you do that, love. Can I just remind you that Hawk and Max risked their lives for you."

"We'll be back for them," Dianna said.

"You keep telling yourself that. As long as your conscience is clear, that's all that matters, eh?"

"That's unfair. What use will I be to you? Especially if you go back into the city?"

What use would Olga be in the city? She didn't know the place. How the hell would she avoid the diseased, cannibals, and warring armies? Again, one word filled Olga's mind. Company. She shook her head and sighed. "You go. You're right, I'll be better off on my own."

A hand rested on Olga's back. It came from Dianna's direction. She twisted away from the girl's touch.

"We'll be watching," Gracie said.

"And what if ..." Olga took a moment. "What if we don't all make it? What if they come here in stages? There's no reason they'll arrive together."

"When you're ready for me to come and get you," Gracie said, "hold up four fingers on your right hand. I'll see that and come. If I see all of you in here, I'll also come."

Olga jumped at the *snap* of the steel door's handle. The hinges cackled again. Not that they had anything to laugh about. Gracie opened the door wide enough for Dianna to leave. "We'll return, okay."

Olga turned her back on them. "I'll believe that when I see it."

Dianna said, "G-goodbye, Olga. See you soon."

The door closed with a *click*, throwing the small space back into complete darkness. After letting go of a hard sigh, Olga's exhaustion caught up with her. She sat cross-legged on the floor, her head in her hands. In spite of herself, she began to cry.

CHAPTER 19

Since William had found the old apartment with Matilda, he'd sat in a corner and hadn't moved. The aches running through his shins and legs had eased, turning into a low buzz of fatigue. They were far enough away from the window to avoid the broken glass on the floor. "How long do you think we've been here for?"

Matilda got to her feet again, squinting as she peered out at the city, searching one way and then the other. "Two hours?" She shrugged. "Maybe more."

It had grown light outside, the grainy hue from the birth of a new day revealing their surroundings to them. Where the darkness hid all its imperfections, the sunlight scrutinised them. The cracks in the walls were putrid scars, the damp plaster inside having swollen and burst through their papery skin. The bare concrete floor, cold and damp, had turned William's bottom numb, but at least it had given him a chance to rest. The previous night had damn near broken him.

His clothes were cold and damp with dew. Another shiver sent a violent spasm through his body.

"Are you okay?"

"I'm as okay as I need to be. It's not like we can do much about that right now."

"What do you mean?"

"We have to move on soon. Much sooner than my body would like."

"But the rest has been good, right? It's helped?"

William winced. "I think so, yeah."

Matilda got to her feet and offered him her hand. She supported most of his weight as he stood and led them over to the window.

Like with the room they were in, the daylight revealed a different city. The imposing blocks and buildings that had loomed over them in the darkness, staring down on them in judgement, were now exposed as decrepit and crumbling forms. "This place looked a lot different when we were running through it last night," William said. "I saw what it used to be. I imagined what the buildings contained inside. But now—"

"It looks like a ghost town," Matilda said.

"Right."

"But didn't Gracie say this place came alive during the day?"

The stamp of boots answered Matilda's question. They echoed through the tight streets.

Both William and Matilda stepped back and used the shadows as cover.

A group of about ten soldiers in red uniform, they dressed like they belonged to the same army, but they lacked any kind of militant co-ordination. They wandered through the city, scanning their surroundings, their identical foot-long metal batons raised and ready to use.

"They look so young," Matilda said.

"Like us when we were sent on our national service."

"At least we had a leader. These lot look like they're making it up as they go along."

"Lambs to the slaughter."

Matilda stepped back another pace and tugged on William's arm. "If the city wakes up like Gracie said it does, I think we should get out of here while it's still early."

The army rounded the next bend, searching the streets but not looking up. They were so wet behind the ears, they'd didn't think to look any higher than their own level. William shook his head. Lambs to the slaughter.

The same bare concrete floor continued into the hallway, the walls as scarred and burst as they'd been in the apartment. Damp chunks of plaster leaked from the deep gashes and spilled across their path. Spiders had made their homes in every corner. Several webs broke on William's face as he walked through them. He pinched at his skin, and despite removing some silk, he couldn't get it all.

The building had a stairwell on one side. Matilda led them to the other. To a window in the far wall. William pointed behind them. "Why not use the stairs?"

Guiding his sight with her pointing hand, Matilda showed William the metal tower in the distance, the landmark Gracie had shown them as their destination. "You think they'll still be there waiting for us?"

"I'm not sure," Matilda said. "But if you have a better plan, I'm all ears. Also"—she stepped from the window onto the steel walkway—"I guessed there'd be one of these fire escapes to climb down. It's a quicker route. The sooner we get to the tower, the better."

They might have only been one floor from the ground, but stepping from the cover of the building exposed them to the wind's full force. It burned William's tired eyes. A clacking called up to them from another street. "Matilda!"

She continued along the metal walkway, her long brown hair streaming out behind her.

Clenched teeth, William hissed, louder this time, "Matilda!"

She halted, and when she turned to look at him, her hair dragged across her face. It took her three attempts to swipe it free before he had her attention. He pointed in the sound's direction, and her features fell slack. William climbed back into the tower.

Matilda joined him. The clacking grew louder. The uneven beat of a mechanical quadruped—of several mechanical quadrupeds—rounded the bend. A pack of dogs. Their eyes glowed red, and their hinged jaws hung open. "I know the last time we saw them they were breathing fire," William said, "but to look at them now. To see them in all their glory makes them—"

"Scarier?"

He nodded. "Scarier. Like I can see the true extent of their power. Thank the heavens they didn't catch us." As the pack passed, William said, "Let's wait for a second. Where there're dogs, there might be more soldiers."

Matilda raised her eyebrows. "Or drones." She peered out at the sky.

Another pack of red-uniformed soldiers rounded the bend. They chased after the dogs. As disorganised as the first lot, they moved like scavengers. Like wild monkeys. Hunched forms, raised weapons. They were here to flush out the enemy, confident because of their numbers.

Matilda shook her head. "Gracie really wasn't exaggerating about the place coming to life, was she?"

It took about a minute for the army to pass. William peered out of the window again, the force of the fresh wind in his face. "I think we're clear for now. You ready for this?"

"I'm not sure ready is the right word, but I can't foresee a better time than now."

When William stood aside, Matilda frowned at him. He shrugged. "You're the one who can see a route through this place. You're a better runner and climber than I am. It makes sense for you to lead."

The deep intake of breath raised Matilda's chest. She leaned forward and kissed William, lingering with their lips pressed together. A half smile. She winked at him. "Are you sure you can keep up?"

"Don't push it."

Matilda stepped from the window, and William followed. Fifteen to twenty feet from the ground, he took another moment in the full force of the cleansing wind.

Light on her feet, Matilda crossed the metal walkway with damn near soundless steps. William's tired body and clumsy gait denied his will to do the same. He moved like a farmer through a muddy field.

The fire escape wobbled with their steps. At what point would it relinquish its grip on the crumbling building?

Matilda jumped half of the last flight, and William followed suit. She landed like a cat. He landed like wet mud.

William checked both ways while remaining on Matilda's tail as she darted down a narrow alley, heading toward Gracie's tower. Only four feet wide, their tight path clung onto the shadows of the previous evening.

Despite Matilda running ahead of him, William saw it first. "Stop!"

She halted at the end of the alley.

The road ahead of them had been ripped up like the one between the three towers. A livid scar streaked through the broken asphalt. The sunlight glinted off a metal disc lying amongst the rubble. "Look."

"A mine," Matilda said. "I didn't see it at all."

Matilda led them around the corner on tiptoes, remaining close to the old shop on their left. A small strip of road close to the building remained intact. They had to trust there were no mines beneath it. They climbed the shop's fire escape. Although why such a short building needed one … surely they could jump from the roof if their lives depended on it.

The roof was only two stories from the ground. The tall metal tower in their sights, Matilda pointed to the building next to them and then the ones leading away from it. "We can get closer to the meeting point via the roofs, but we have to take a longer route." She shrugged. "Better that than being torn to shreds by an exploding mine, eh?"

More footsteps below. William walked to the edge of the roof, his steps crunching over the layer of white gravel covering it. He peered over. A group of red-uniformed soldiers came from the same alley they'd passed through. They pinned themselves to the wall and followed the same path William and Matilda had. "Are they following us?"

Matilda drew a breath to reply, but the *tock* of steps against the metal fire escape said it for her. She mouthed the word, *Shit!*

Matilda led the way, jumping across the small gap over the alley they and the soldiers had used. But instead of taking off across the next roof, she dropped to her front and shimmied up against a lip about a foot tall around the edge of the building.

William copied her, the gravel on the flat roof digging into his chest. It made sense. If they continued running, the soldiers would see them. But how could they defend themselves when they lay on their bellies?

Crunching steps signalled the first of the soldiers had made it to the roof. Could they outrun them if they needed to? Could William? Matilda could outrun most people, especially up high. Maybe they could shove them back if they jumped over. Only a two-storey fall, but it would at least slow them down.

"You say you heard something?" one of the soldiers said.

William's heart slammed in his chest, and he chased his shallow breaths.

"I dunno," a deeper voice replied. "Maybe I imagined it."

The soldiers continued to walk towards the spot William and Matilda hid in. Slow and torturous, the steps closed in on them.

"You found anything?" A girl's voice this time. Farther away than the others. Maybe she remained on the fire escape.

The shadows of the two boys leaned over them, stretching across onto the next roof. An inverse spotlight searching for the enemy. William lay tense, his hands balled. If they jumped across, he'd be ready.

"No," the deeper voice said, and one shadow withdrew. "Nothing."

The second shadow followed the first. The crunch of their steps back across the small stones on the roof. The *tock* of their retreat against the metal stairs, they headed back to the ground.

William waited for Matilda. She poked her head over the wall and stood up. "Come on, let's go." She took off again across the rooftops. The alleys between each one stretched only a few feet at a time. Easy enough to cross, even for William.

Several rooftops behind her, Matilda rested her hands on her hips and puffed as she walked to the edge of the next building. "We've gone as far as we can without going to ground." She looked one way down the street and then the other. She ran to the other side and did the same. When she came back to William, she shook her head. "There aren't any fire escapes. *None* of these buildings has one."

"So we have to go back?"

Matilda returned to the edge of the building and peered over. "Do you trust me?"

"With all my heart."

"Then follow me." Matilda slid off the roof backwards and hung down. A six-inch-thick metal pipe ran straight to the ground. She kicked it twice. It held. She hooked her feet around it and then grabbed on with one hand and then the other.

Backflips turned through William's stomach when she let go of the roof's edge. She shimmied down the pipe an inch at a time. She'd lowered herself about six feet when she reached out her right leg. At full stretch, she caught the window ledge leading to the first floor. Her right arm next, she clung on with her fingertips. She stretched between the pipe and the window like a star.

William yelled when Matilda kicked away from the pipe and swung out like a loose door before she pulled herself in through the first-floor window.

At some point the adrenaline had to run out. And of course that would happen when he needed it most. While hanging from the roof, William's aches returned with full force. His knuckles burned under the strain of his weight. He caught the drainpipe with one foot and then the other before reaching down and clamping onto the thick metal pole with both hands. The wind tugged on his clothes as he shimmied down, Matilda watching him from the safety of the building's first floor.

Battling his own trembling body, it might not have been far to the hard asphalt below, but it would still hurt if he fell. William stretched his leg across and caught the window ledge. His height should have given him an advantage over Matilda, but he didn't have a shred of her skill or confidence.

When William reached over and caught the inside of the window frame, Matilda stroked the back of his hand. The reassurance he needed. He kicked away from the pipe, swung out like Matilda had, and whimpered as he pulled himself into the building's first floor.

Matilda beamed and threw her arms around him. "Well done." She kissed the side of his face five or six times before she let go. "Now let's get moving."

The stairs inside the building were made from concrete. Once downstairs, Matilda led them to the road. The same road they'd avoided crossing because of the mines. The layer of asphalt on this section remained mostly intact, the cracks too small to have mines in them. "Do we trust it?" she said.

William shrugged.

"I can't make this decision on my own."

"Sorry, you're right." William led the charge, sprinting across the road, checking left and right as he ran. He charged down another alley and halted at the end, another wide street separating them and a row of shops.

"They've got fire escapes on them," Matilda said.

"You think we should go on the roofs again?"

"It gives us a better vantage point and takes us closer to what looks like the final row of shops before we get to Gracie's tower. You want me to lead?"

"Sure."

Matilda crossed the road and climbed. William followed. The metal stairs shook with their ascent.

Several of the buildings they crossed had statues on their roofs. From a large faded *M* to a chicken, to a donut with teeth marks along one side. They reached the building with the donut. They were as close to the tower as they could be without going back to ground.

Matilda walked to the edge of the roof and stepped back before William reached her.

"What is it?"

Her face pale, Matilda pointed down to their left. An army gathered in the street below. This time they wore blue. About one hundred of them, they had drones hovering nearby.

"Why have they chosen to have their meeting there?" William said.

"I'm not sure that's the question we need to be asking."

"How do we get them to go away?"

Matilda nodded. "How indeed?"

CHAPTER 20

William pulled Matilda back from the edge of the roof and guided her so they both crouched behind the huge sun-bleached donut. A line of flat roofs broken by narrow alleys stretched away from them in both directions. It gave them options. He tugged on Matilda's arm and said, "Follow me."

William crossed from one roof to the next, passing the garish statues raised in honour of each shop's wares. They passed a large *M*, a fifteen-foot-tall chicken, a floating smile. Although there seemed very little to grin about in this savage city.

Every step took them farther away from Gracie's tower and deeper into the ruins they so desperately wanted behind them. But they had no chance against the army below and had to do something. William led them back to the fire escape they'd used to get to the roofs. He led them back across the roads and towards the mines buried amongst the churned asphalt.

"Why are we back here?" Matilda said.

William lifted a chunk of the broken road and tucked it beneath his arm. Still several feet from the exposed mine, yet he watched it without blinking as if the inanimate object might give him feedback other than its binary existence of dormant or explode. "I have a plan." He climbed the same fire escape they'd used to avoid the mines the first time they were here. The one the red soldiers had followed them up. He stood aside to let Matilda pass.

"What—"

William threw the chunk of asphalt into the centre of the road.

Matilda had already taken off by the time it triggered the mine. A *whomp* of ignition followed by an atmosphere-rending *crack* from the explosion. It shook the ground, but the buildings stood strong.

The charge of the blue army descended on the explosion site, their footsteps closing in.

Matilda slowed to let William run at her side. Her face red, she turned her palms to the sky. "Where are we going?"

"Back to where we were."

They reached the roof they'd climbed from previously. Matilda pointed at the edge. "You want to slide down that pipe again?"

"Yeah, and back to the roof with the donut. Hopefully, this'll move Fear's army and give us our chance to cross." The first of Fear's soldiers emerged. "Get down!" He pulled on her shoulder, and they both dropped to their fronts.

Fifteen to twenty soldiers appeared. Matilda said, "Is that it?"

William said, "I kinda hoped they'd all come."

The soldiers peered one way and then the other. They spoke amongst themselves, but they were too far away for

William to hear their words. They shrugged and shook their heads. They left.

"What the ...?" William said. "So much for *that* plan. What are we going to do now?"

Matilda stood up.

"Where are you going?"

"Back to the donut. We still need to get to Gracie's tower, and that's a better place to wait than here. Surely we'll get a chance to cross at some point." She kneeled down and turned her back to the road. She lay on her front and dropped her legs over the edge of the roof. The pipe rang from where she struck it with her foot. She lowered herself, more graceful this time for having already done it once before.

William did his best to hide his trembling form. After all, he had planned this route. His knuckles ached as much this time as they had previously. But he'd done it once before, he could do it again. A few feet down the pipe, he stretched his leg for the window, hooked his right foot around the edge, and grabbed on with his right hand. For the second time, he swung away from the building and pulled himself inside in one fluid movement.

They wasted no time, running to the ground floor again, crossing the road again, and ducking into the alley they'd used the last time they ran through here again. This time, Matilda led them the entire way, across the next road and up the fire escape, back to the row of buildings with statues on the roofs.

But when she reached the top of the first escape, she waited.

"What is it?" William said.

She cupped her ear. "Hear that?"

Distant, yet distinct. *Clack, clack. Clack, clack.* "The dogs?"

Matilda nodded.

"Fury are coming to check out the explosion?"
She nodded again.
William smiled. "This might be our ticket out of here."

CHAPTER 21

The dogs' clacking steps in the lead, Fury's soldiers behind them. It sounded like there were far more of them than had been sent to investigate from Fear's side. A road and a row of buildings between them, William could only track them by sound. They arrived at the explosion site in stages, several groups converging on that one point. "How many do you think there are?"

Matilda shook her head. "Hard to say. But if they run into Fear's army, I'm guessing they'll be outnumbered." She dropped to her front and crawled to the other side of the roof, peering down on where the blue-uniformed soldiers waited.

When she returned, William said, "They're still not moving?"

Matilda shook her head. "How can they not know they're there? Surely they've heard them?"

"And what if Fury's army also decides there's nothing to investigate and goes back the other way?"

Matilda said, "We have to do something."

The building they were currently on had a lip similar to

the one they'd lain behind when they'd hidden from Fury's soldiers. A foot tall and thick, it ran around the building's perimeter. Topped with concrete slabs, many of which were cracked, dividing them into smaller chunks. William pulled the corner of one free. The heavy lump about the size of his palm. A road and a row of buildings separated them from Fury's army. Fear were on the road behind them. The two warring cities separated by one empty street. Matilda pulled on his arm.

"It's okay," William said. "I've got this." He launched the chunk of concrete at the row of buildings opposite. He hit a pipe similar to the one they'd climbed down when they had no fire escape. And he hit it true. The contact struck it like a bell.

Matilda leaped from their current building to the next, taking them closer to the one with the donut on the roof. William followed, and they both dropped to their fronts two buildings away. They lay in the shadow of the smiling face.

"Do you think it wor—"

Clack-clack. Clack-clack.

The first of the dogs appeared in the central road, Fury's army on their tail.

"You were right," William said. "They're well outnumbered."

"Speaking of which." Matilda pointed down the road to their right. A solitary soldier dressed in blue. From the roar in the street below, Fury's army saw him too. They charged, Fear's soldier running back to regroup with his comrades.

"I feel sorry for them," William said. "They've no idea what we've led them into."

"You can feel sorry for them when we're out of here. Gracie said how these two cities are constantly at war. Them coming together is inevitable, whether we had a hand in it or not."

The blue soldier vanished, and the red army followed him, the dogs leading the charge.

A deafening roar a few seconds later.

"Looks like they've found each other. Come on." Matilda jumped to her feet again and led him across the roofs.

Past the giant chicken and the large *M*, William and Matilda reached the donut again. The *whoosh* of flames met the stuttered bursts of bullet fire. They crawled to the edge of the roof. Most of Fury's army had already retreated. A line of lunatics stood as their last defence.

The lunatics fell with twitches and convulsions, the drones' bullets mowing them down, opening the way for Fear's army to give chase.

William pointed across the road at Gracie's metal tower. "I think this is our moment."

"You want me to go first?"

He shook his head. "Let me."

The neighbouring building had a fire escape that led to the alley between the two shops. William hopped across the gap and took it. Screams, bullet fire, and the roar of flames drowned out his and Matilda's metallic steps.

At the end of the alley, Matilda behind him, he peered out to the left. The soldiers had gone for now. They wouldn't get a better chance than this. He sprinted across the road towards the metal tower and yanked the creaking steel door wide.

A blinking Olga stared up at him. A confused frown and bloodshot eyes. Breathless, William said, "We need to go now."

"Wha—"

"*Now*, Olga!"

A flash of fire ignited in her ochre glare, but she shelved her rage. She stood up on shaking legs and stumbled out into the bright glow of a new day.

Matilda led the way back across the road, back down the alley they'd emerged from, and back to the fire escape to the roof with the donut.

Still half asleep and her hair dishevelled, Olga had creases on her cheeks from where she must have lain on the hard floor. Viewing the world through a tight squint, she shrugged and scratched her head. "You wanna tell me what's going on?"

"There's a war being fought down there," William said.

"I can hear that."

"We started it."

"Huh?"

"The blue army," Matilda said. "Fear's army. They were gathered outside the tower."

Olga's already pale face lost even more colour.

"We had to lure them away to get to you," William said. "That's why we had to get out of there urgently. They might come back. Where are the others?"

Olga sneered. "Gracie left."

"What?" William said.

"She went to her community and took Dianna with her."

"And Artan?" Matilda said.

"Max, Artan, and Hawk got separated from us. Hawk was being a hero again, trying to fight the diseased when he should have run."

William shook his head. "What a moron."

"Exactly."

Screams rang through the city. The burst of gunfire, the whoosh of flames, the cries of people dying.

"So Gracie just left?" Matilda said. "She left when my brother needed her?"

"She said she couldn't wait any longer, and the fact that you and William, and then Hawk and the others, didn't follow her lead wasn't a reason for her to risk her life by waiting around. You know how I feel about the woman, but I can't blame her." Olga pointed at the tower. "There's a camera in that tower."

"A what?" William said.

"It's a device that allows them to see into the tower from their community."

"What the …?"

Olga shrugged. "I know. Anyway, she said she watches it, and when we're all waiting, she'll come and get us."

"And if we don't all make it out?" William said. Even suggesting it elicited a hard glare from Matilda.

"She said we should hold up four fingers on our right hand. That'll tell her we're ready to get out of here."

"So what do we do?" Matilda said.

"What else can we do?" Olga said.

"We should find the others. They might need our help."

"And if we don't find them?" Olga said.

"We come back here. They know where they need to get to. At least looking for them will give us something to do."

Olga pointed up the street. "Going to war with those armies will give us something to do; that doesn't mean we should do it."

"You'd rather sit around here waiting for them to turn up? The way I see it," Matilda said, "very little's changed with our plan. We need to get to that tower as a group and then head to Gracie's community. We only do something different if we have good reason. So we're agreed? We find the others?"

William shrugged. "Yeah."

Olga looked from William to Matilda. "I suppose it's better than doing nothing. But I think we should stay close to the tower so we don't miss them. They might find their way here without our help."

CHAPTER 22

Max panted as he ran. A new day had begun, and none of them had rested. And now this. Three dogs and five soldiers on their tail. The dogs drove them on with their searing heat. If they got any closer, they'd fuse his shirt to his back. The diseased he could deal with, even if Hawk had been an idiot charging into a fight with them, but he didn't have an immunity to fire. Or to being battered with a metal club by Fury's army.

His hands were slick with diseased blood, his right palm stinging with cuts from the rock he'd used to bludgeon them. They'd charged only a handful of the creatures, but as soon as they'd engaged them in battle, more arrived. By the time they'd finished, over one hundred rancid bodies lay scattered on the ground, their vinegar tang palpable in the air. Every creature Max took down stared at him through familiar eyes and hissed his name. *Mad Max.* He saw Cyrus too many times to count.

And then the dogs and soldiers arrived. Not as fast as Artan, Max ran with Hawk beside him while Matilda's brother led their retreat.

Like when they'd followed Gracie, Artan ducked into buildings, jumped walls, and dived through old windows. Shattered glass, debris, and dust kicked up at their feet. From one building to the next, they weaved through a life long forgotten.

Many of the larger window frames had low walls. It made the boys' path easy, for now. For both them and the five soldiers with their dogs.

Max yelled, "We need a better solution than this, Artan."

"What do you think I'm looking for?" Artan turned right when he jumped out of the next shop.

The army and dogs had only been on their tail for a few minutes. The next few minutes mattered even more. They passed another fire escape on their right. "What are you waiting for?" Max said.

"A space we can defend."

Another *whomp* of igniting flames. Max ruffled his nose at the acrid reek of his own singed hair. Their lead had halved from thirty to fifteen feet. If Artan didn't decide where to go soon, then he would.

After a quick double take, Artan turned left into an alley. Max and Hawk followed.

A flight of stairs in front of them. But unlike the fire escapes, this flight led in one straight line to a steel door on the first floor of a building. Otherwise it would have been a dead end. Artan leaped mid-climb and landed two-footed on the other side of the missing stairs.

At least the day had broken. They would have had no chance in the dark. Max leaped across the six-foot gap next. He landed on the other side, his right foot buckling beneath him. His leg folded, he slammed down on his knee, and he fell forward.

Hawk directly behind him, the hunter leaped, tripped,

and belly-flopped on Max's back. The weight of his stocky frame forced Max into the stairs and drove the wind from him. Hawk climbed over him as the *clack-clack* of the first dog began its ascent.

While Hawk scrambled clear, the dog leaped. Max pulled his legs away from the edge. Just a few feet between him and the dog's glowing red eyes. It snapped its jaw with a *crack!* A token effort, the metallic beast twisted in mid-air as it plummeted to the ground with a *clang!*

The other two dogs learned fast. They waited at the bottom of the stairs.

Stumbling after his friends, Max met them at the steel door. The door without a handle.

Hawk kicked it. The force of his attack, combined with the door's refusal to budge, sent him stumbling back. He threw his arms up. "It's been welded shut."

"How—" Max caught his breath "—are we supposed to get through?"

Until that moment, Artan had been the one with all the ideas. He shrugged.

"What the fuck, Hawk?" Max said.

"What? I didn't lead us here."

"Why did you charge those diseased? Why be a hero?"

"I was trying to help."

"By doing what? What did you achieve? You think you can kill every diseased on the planet?"

"There were only a few of them. I thought I'd get to them before they got to us."

"We could have gone the other way. We didn't have to fight them. Had you not been driven by your ego and pride, we would all be in that tower right now, waiting for William and Matilda to catch up with us. As it is, we're going to die in this shitty alley. And for what?"

The fire left Hawk's eyes and he lowered his gaze.

Fury's soldiers, five of them dressed in red, waited at the end of the alley. The three metal dogs paced. A tall man with a shaved head, the leader of the group, stepped forward. "We won't follow you up there. We're not stupid."

"What will you do, then?" Artan said.

"Wait. We'll wait."

Hawk brandished his knife, the blade covered in diseased blood. "You'll be waiting a long time."

"We have an army behind us. If we have to do this in shifts, then so be it." A wicked smile split the man's angular face. "We can wait forever. What will you do when you get hungry? Or we could just come back with spears. Rocks. Throwing knives."

Max's stomach sank.

"So you might as well come down now. If you do, we'll go easy on you. We'll just cut your throats and leave you for the scavengers. I mean, we might string up your corpses as a reminder to anyone that this is our city, but you'll be dead, so what does it matter, right?"

Artan muttered beneath his breath, "Fuck!"

Max said, "And all of this because you took us into a fight we didn't need to have."

Hawk shook his head. "You're right. This is my fault. I'm going to go down and face them."

"What?" Artan said.

"It'll give you and Max a chance to get away."

"No, it won't." Artan shook his head. "It will give them a chance to kill you on your own; then they'll only have to wait for two of us to come down. We've got nowhere to run."

Hawk's broad shoulders sagged. "Arthur."

Max said it this time. "What?"

"That's what he called me. Grandfather Jacks. He named

me Arthur. He said I was useless, that I'd amount to nothing." Tears filled Hawk's eyes, and his knife shook in his tight grip. "He said I was a liability and that he needed to teach me lessons on how to be better. But I never learned from his teaching, so he taught me again"—his eyes glazed—"and again, and again." He launched his knife at the soldiers. They moved aside, the *ting* of the blade hitting the ground. "See! I'm useless. I can't even throw a knife."

"Look." Max put a hand on Hawk's back. The hunter jumped at first, but then his gaze settled. "Whatever happens, we're going to find a way out of this. *Whatever* happens."

Hawk nodded several times and bowed his head.

Artan peered over Hawk and raised his eyebrows at Max. "So what do we do, then?"

"You led us here," Max said.

"We still need a way out," Artan said. "Regardless of who's to blame."

The roofs of the buildings were too high to reach, even if they stood on one another's shoulders like when they got out of the pit in the funnel. The soldiers and the dogs waited, staring up at them, batons raised, jaws hanging open. Max yelled and kicked the welded door again. Another deep *thud!* "This thing sounds like it's several feet thick. Maybe we have to fight them."

Artan shook his head. "There must be a better option."

As one, the dogs' eyes switched from red to blue. Max said, "Are you seeing that?"

"Uh-huh," Artan said.

All three dogs turned and ran.

The soldier with the bald head pointed up at Max, Artan, and Hawk. "Know that you got lucky today. And if you have any sense, you'd get the hell out of this city right now." His jaw clenched and his teeth bared, he said, "If we find you again, that promise of a quick death has expired. We *will* fuck you up."

The tall soldier led his team after the dogs.

About thirty seconds passed before Hawk said, "Do you really think they've gone?"

"Are you still keen to go down there?" Max said.

"Max!" Artan tilted his head to one side.

"What?"

"We can't make him go down there on his own."

"Not on his own," Max said. "Just first. We wouldn't be in this shit if it wasn't for him. It's the least he can do."

Before Artan replied, Hawk raised a halting hand. "He's right. It is the least I can do."

Much easier going down than it had been going up, Hawk crossed the gap in the stairs from a two-footed standing jump. He landed on the other side with a *clang!* His fists raised in front of him, he descended the stairs with slow and deliberate steps.

Clang! Max followed Hawk.

Clang! Artan took up the rear.

At the end of the alley, Hawk charged out into the road, picked up his knife, and slashed at the air. He turned one way and then the other, his blade out in front of him. "They've gone."

"Where?" Artan said.

"How would I know?" Hawk shrugged. "I'm guessing what happened to the dogs meant something? Maybe it was a call for help. All that matters is they've gone. Now let's get out of here before they come back."

Max led Artan from the alleyway. He pointed at the tall steel tower in the distance. "Let's take this blessing for what it is and get to Gracie's tower."

"You suddenly gone religious?" Artan said. "Praise be to the high father and all that?"

Thick lines creased Hawk's brow, and his eyes darkened, his irises turning black.

"Sorry." Artan raised his hands in apology. "I didn't think."

"Look, let's just get out of here," Hawk said, "before they come back." He led them in the opposite direction to the one taken by the red army.

CHAPTER 23

William followed the same route as Olga and Matilda. He hung from the first floor of the fire escape and dropped to the ground. He landed beside them, absorbing the shock with bent knees. "That many soldiers in one place has to be a good thing, right?"

Olga raised an eyebrow. "Unless you run into them."

"Well, *obviously*, but at least we know where a good chunk of them are. And we're going the other way, aren't we?"

"We are." Olga checked up and down the wide road and led them out of there.

"How do you know your way already?" William said, following Olga down another tight alley. "Everywhere looks the same."

"I don't trust Gracie, so I paid attention to where she led us. You can never be too careful, can you?"

"Apparently not."

At the end of every alley, Olga had done the same thing, this one no different. She paused, poked her head into the road, looked one way and then the other, and led them out. Although, unlike every other occasion, this time the city opened up, a large mall in front of them. A vast and ugly building. It took up more space than it had any right to. Made predominantly from rusting steel, it had once been painted white, but most of the paint had since peeled off.

They closed in on the derelict metal monstrosity, crossing the open plain of asphalt that surrounded it on every side. Like every other road in the area, nature had begun its reclamation of the land. Cracks dominated the black surface. Shoots of green packed each one, grassy tendrils of enquiry before they swamped the city for good. What would this place look like in fifty years' time? How long had it taken to get to this state?

"Gracie told us a bit more about this place after we'd lost the drone. She called this the car park," Olga said, all three of them jogging side by side. "Apparently, people drove large metal vehicles, came here on their days off, and spent their time walking around the shops, buying shit they didn't need. It seems like a waste of a life to me."

Matilda shook her head. "I don't get it either. And this is where you last saw—"

"Over there," Olga said. She pointed at a wide sprawl of dead diseased. "Jeez, I didn't realise there were that many. Hawk and the others went one way, Gracie, Dianna, and myself went the other. They must have drawn them out into the open to make them easier to fight."

Many of the corpses had glistening holes, puncture wounds from Hawk's and Artan's knives. Many more had smashed-in skulls and distorted faces. They'd been bludgeoned by something hard and angular. "What was Hawk playing at?" William said. "There must be a hundred of them."

Olga shrugged. "I'm not sure even Hawk could answer that question. Although, to be fair to him, from where we stood, there was no telling how many there were. Also, by the look of things, it probably won't help our cause to get him to wind his neck in when we do reunite with them."

"What do you mean?" William said.

"Well, if this is anything to go by, it looks like the three of them got away. Hawk went to war and won. That might make it much harder to convince him his actions were reckless. And I doubt he's aware of the impact on Max." Olga looked away from the pile of bodies, her eyes losing focus.

"Look!" Matilda pointed at the ground. The twisted and savaged corpses lay in a lake of their own blood. Crimson footsteps led away from it, the early morning light revealing a shining trail.

"Well, at least we know which way they went," William said. He rested a hand on Olga's back. "We can help Max when we find him. Hopefully, we'll be able to rest up in Gracie's community. Come on, let's go."

Olga gulped and nodded. She took the lead again. They followed the shining footsteps towards the large mall.

"Please tell me they didn't go back in there," William said.

The steps had grown fainter the farther away they were from the bloody mess of diseased. "It doesn't look like they did," Matilda said. Almost invisible, she pointed at the faintly glistening remnants of their path out of there. It caught the light like a slug trail. "I think they went around."

The first building in the next street stood as an enormous cube with a roof. Each side stretched at least one hundred feet long. A functional building, aesthetics be damned. "It reminds me of the barns in Edin," William said. "A place built for storage. Dad took me—" A lump swelled in his throat, robbing him of his words.

"It has a fire escape," Olga said. "We should get on top of it and see if we can see the boys."

William coughed to clear the lump in his throat. His eyes itched with the start of tears.

Matilda said, "Just lead the way and we'll follow."

The wall of the building made from bare red brick, it had small windows in it that looked like they were there for ventilation. When they finally reached a window they could peer into, Olga poked her head inside.

She snapped back so quickly, William jumped, teetering on the edge of his balance, his heels hanging over the last stair he'd climbed. Olga's face had turned several shades paler. "What is it?" William said.

Olga stepped aside so William could look in. He approached on tiptoes and held his breath as he peered into the warehouse. A chill snaked through him. As he pulled away, he mouthed one word at Olga. *Fuck!*

CHAPTER 24

The inside of the building had been as William had expected. A vast open space without walls. It had been designed for storage. Although, he hadn't expected to find the entire first floor covered with sleeping bodies. At least, they all appeared to be asleep. Many of them snored and grunted while they dozed, some of them entangled on the floor, lying across one another like post-coital lovers. The place reeked of rot, dirt, and flatulence. The collective funk of a warehouse filled with scavengers.

Olga hissed, "There must be four hundred of them in there." She backed away.

"And that's on the first floor," William said.

Olga pointed down. "You think there's more below?"

"Who knows." William shrugged. "Hopefully not, and hopefully that's all of them in the city. But what concerns me more is how there're enough bodies to keep them all fed."

"What concerns me more is why we're still waiting here." Matilda pointed down the stairs they'd just climbed. "Can we have this conversation somewhere else?" Her eyes widened. "*Anywhere* else."

Olga led them away, their steps far more cautious on the way down than they'd been on the way up. As they got closer to the ground, they quickened their retreat. The scavengers might have lived off scraps in this city, but they preferred their dinner with a pulse.

Their quickened steps turned into a flat-out sprint when they hit the ground. Olga ran around the back of the warehouse and across a road before she took them down another alley, and deeper into the more built-up part of the city.

She ran to escape, but William called ahead, "Olga, you need to slow down."

"Did you see them back there?"

"Of course, but I don't think they saw us. We need to keep our heads and make sure we don't run into more trouble. Maybe we should assume *every* building is occupied, and *every* corner crowded with either Fear's or Fury's armies. Gracie said this city was a very different place during the day."

Olga scowled at William's invocation of Gracie, but she dipped her head in a nod of concession. "I've no idea where Max and the others might be, but I'd say we need to get on the roofs to stand a better chance of spotting them and any other danger."

"Do you think they might have gone to the tower?" Matilda said. "I think we should head back that way now."

Olga pointed to her right. "The tower's over there. If we travel towards it across the roofs, we can do a lot from high up. Two birds and all that."

When neither William nor Matilda responded, Olga climbed the closest fire escape. She moved slower and with more deliberate steps than when they'd climbed up the side of the warehouse. At the first window, she peered in. A few seconds of her scanning the darkness, she gave William a thumbs up and moved on. William followed, throwing only a cursory glance into the empty building as he passed the same window.

Nothing to block the wind on the roof, it rocked William back on his heels, his fatigue robbing him of his stability. Many of the buildings in this part of the city were similar. Small two-storey cubes with flat roofs covered in white pebbles and moss. They were packed so tightly together, to cross from one to the next required only a large step, even for Olga's small legs. "Gracie was right about this place being built to last."

"How long do you think it will be before the buildings start collapsing?" Matilda said.

Olga rolled her eyes. "While this is all very interesting"—she pointed at Gracie's tower—"we need to get back. While we run across these roofs, I recommend you and William run down one side while I run down the other. That way we can scan for danger." She'd chosen the right side, the side that overlooked the road separating them from the scavengers' warehouse. "Let's get moving, yeah?"

Several buildings later, Olga stopped. William grabbed Matilda's arm, halting her before he pointed at the short girl. "She's found something."

The gravel crunched beneath their steps as they joined Olga on the other side. She led their eyes with her pointing finger.

Matilda said it first. "Oh, fuck!"

Max, Hawk, and Artan. They were close to the warehouse.

Matilda hopped up and down on the spot, waving her arms.

Olga pulled them down. "Stop!"

Her hands gripped as tight fists at her side, Matilda stepped closer to Olga. "What did you do that for?"

"Look!"

"Oh, shit!" William said. Ten to fifteen blue soldiers had gathered in the road, close to the boys, but they faced the other way. The boys saw them and retreated into the alley running alongside the warehouse.

"Talk about a rock and a hard place," William said. "How will we help them get out of this without the scavengers seeing them?"

"We have to warn them." Matilda took off without consultation, retracing their path back across the rooftops.

But before Matilda reached the fire escape they'd climbed, she halted. William caught up to her and followed her guidance when she pointed. More of Fear's soldiers. There were now about fifty in total. They split up, most of them closing in on the end of the alley the boys had vanished down. About ten others cut through another path to block off their escape at the other end. Four drones remained with the larger army. They were also trained on the alley's exit.

"It's a trap," Matilda said. "They're going to send the smaller group around the back to chase them into the larger group. We need to tell them."

Olga pulled Matilda from the edge of the roof. "And give ourselves away in the process?" She pointed at her temple. "You need to think, Matilda. We let them know we're up here and none of us are walking away from this."

"Besides," William said, "we know Hawk and they don't."

"What do you mean?" Olga said.

"Most people would run away from the smaller army and get funnelled into the larger pack. Their best chance of getting out of this is to charge rather than run."

Placing her hands together as if in prayer, Olga said, "For once, Hawk, please try to be a hero."

CHAPTER 25

Max bit his tongue and let Hawk speak. He at least needed to hear him out.

"There was only a handful of them," Hawk said. "I say we should attack them before they attack us."

Max rolled his eyes. At least he'd listened. "When has you charging in helped us so far? When you tried to save Olga on the roof of the tower, you nearly got her and yourself killed. When you charged in to fight the diseased—"

"We beat them, didn't we?"

Max dragged air in through his nose. "Did *we?* Mad Max. He shook his head to rid his mind's eye of Cyrus' face. "Regardless of who killed what"—his right palm still buzzed with the small cuts from the jagged rock he'd chosen as his weapon—"we didn't need to fight them, *and* we got separated from the others. We wouldn't even be having this conversation had we made a better choice. We'd be with the others in Gracie's tower. Or maybe even resting up at Gracie's community."

"But we *are* having the conversation." Hawk's upper body

tensed. "If we neutralise the threat, we take control. You can see I've been trying to help, right, Artan?"

Artan's lips tightened. "You might have been trying …"

"But—"

"I hate to say this, Hawk"—Max pointed away from them to the other end of the alley—"but I'm going this way. You can come if you like. It's your call. I won't risk my life unnecessarily for you again."

Hawk's internal battle played out on his features. It started with a hard scowl, which wavered, his glare softening. "Fine. Whatever. You lead."

Max led them down the alley, away from the army they'd avoided. They walked between a large warehouse on their left and a smaller shop on their right. Just getting his body to respond took a great effort. Between Edin, the Asylum, and now this city, he'd fought a lifetime's worth of battles and more. If only he could find somewhere to rest. At the very least, they needed to avoid any more conflict. Hopefully, when they finally got to Gracie's tower, Olga and the others would be waiting for them.

As he closed in on the end of the alley, Max turned back to Artan and Hawk. He pointed over to his right. "We're going to head that way for a few blocks to get us closer to the tower. Any ob—"

Over the heads of Artan and Hawk, Max saw Olga, Matilda, and William. They stood on the roof of one of the buildings closer to the end of the alley they were avoiding. Olga's lips were pursed, her eyes sad. What did she know?

Max raised his hand to wave, dropping it the second footsteps appeared behind him. Hawk and Artan reached back for their knives, but halted when the tip of a blade bit into Max's neck. It was like they felt it too.

A deep male voice said, "Get on your knees and I might let you live for a few more hours."

Artan and Hawk dropped. Max followed a second later. The unforgiving road hurt his kneecaps.

"I told you we should have fought the others," Hawk said.

The brilliant glow from several drones appeared at the other end of the alley. Even in daylight, their strong glare damn near blinded Max. They'd run away from about ten soldiers, but now there were roughly forty of them, blocking off their exit. He could only guess at how many were behind him.

Hawk looked back. When he turned around, his shoulders slumped and he dropped his head. Whichever way they'd chosen, they were screwed.

CHAPTER 26

"You need to calm down," William said.

Olga pointed to where Max, Hawk, and Artan were being led away, her eyes wide. "But we need to go *now*."

"We need to think this through. Did you see how many of them were down there?"

"That's *exactly* why we have to help them. We might have the element of surprise if we attack now."

Matilda said, "The element of surprise isn't a panacea, Olga. They outnumber us fifteen to one. We want to get to them as much as you do, but you were the one who said we have an advantage if we don't reveal ourselves until the right time."

"That was before *they* got captured."

"They don't know we exist," William said, "and we need to keep it that way until the time's right."

Olga bounced on the spot, throwing glances in the direction the army had gone with their three friends. "But Max is down there. It's all right for you, you have Matilda up here with you."

"I still care about the others."

Matilda said, "And what about Artan?"

"Yet you still agree with him?" Olga said.

Matilda shrugged. "I want to get them free as much as you do, but I can't see what we'll accomplish by rushing in. What use are we to them if we all get caught? Maybe if I saw an angle, I'd be up for risking it, but no matter how you look at their situation, in this moment there's nothing we can do for them. First, we need to follow them. We need to find out where they're going."

Olga burst away from them, breaking into a jog, but William caught her before she stepped out of reach, grabbing her arm and pulling her back.

A raised fist, her teeth clenched, Olga said, "What the fuck are you doing? You said we should follow them!"

"Come on, Olga." William shook her. "Get your head together. You're pissed off with Hawk for charging into things without thinking." He flinched when Matilda grabbed his arm. She pointed away from them. About ten more soldiers dressed in blue were heading their way at a jog.

Olga lowered her fist. Her tight jaw loosened.

William dropped onto his front on the small white stones and crawled on his stomach towards the edge of the building.

Olga slid up next to him.

Matilda ran away from them across the roofs, tracking the path of the main army, a road and a row of buildings separating them.

The newest group of soldiers entered the alley Max, Artan, and Hawk had walked down. Olga raised her eyebrows at William, who nodded. They remained on their fronts while the soldiers followed the path of their friends.

The slightest crunch of her steps, Matilda rejoined William and Olga.

"Now imagine if we'd followed the first lot," William said.

"All right." Olga scowled at him. "I get your point."

When the soldiers vanished from sight, William and the other two stood up. Matilda led them, tracking the smaller pack. They caught glimpses of them between the buildings. Enough to keep tabs on their progress.

The scream caught William off guard and forced him to a halt. Shrill and blood-curdling, the woman's cry echoed through the city.

The trailing group of soldiers paused at the end of an alley, giving William, Matilda, and Olga an unobstructed view. They'd caught a girl in a red uniform.

"That must have been what they were chasing," William said.

The girl screamed and shook, twisting and turning against the restraint of one of the larger men in the pack. Her hair fell across her face with her futile struggle. She flicked her head back, trying to slam it into the nose of the man restraining her. The girl then stamped her foot on top of the blue soldier's right boot. The soldier screamed and momentarily let her go.

The girl broke free, charging down the alley towards William and the others. But the soldiers gave chase. One caught up and kicked her feet from beneath her.

The girl managed two more wild steps, running while leaning forward, her arms flailing. She hit the ground hard, her palms scraping along the road as she tried to cushion her fall. Tears ran down her cheeks, and her mouth twisted with her grief as the blue soldiers surrounded her. She rolled over onto her back and placed her hands together as if in prayer, her face puce. "Please. I've done nothing wrong. Please let me go."

One of Fear's female soldiers ran forward and kicked the girl in the face. The loud *crack* snapped William's shoulders into his neck, and he winced as the others went to work on her. They jeered and spat, taking turns to slap, kick, and punch her.

"Why don't they just fucking kill her?" Olga said.

"That would be too simple." Matilda's eyes narrowed. "They want to break her. They want to destroy what that red uniform symbolises."

The next thirty seconds lasted a lifetime. They beat the girl limp. The two largest soldiers then took an ankle each and dragged her down the road, her uniform riding up, her back scraping against the rough asphalt. They headed in the same direction the others had taken Hawk, Max, and Artan.

Olga ran to the edge of the roof, dropped off the side onto the metal fire escape, and jogged down the stairs.

Matilda raised her eyebrows. William shrugged. "At least she waited until we can get down there without being seen." He followed, dropping from the roof to the metal walkway, his steps far from soundless, but hopefully quiet enough for them not to find the ears of the blue soldiers.

Olga reached the ground and took off across the road. She vanished down an alley. The way seemed clear, so William followed, Matilda a few steps behind.

Like many of the alleys in this part of the ruined city, the walls were close and the shadows deep. Windows without panes on either side provided a view into the abandoned shops.

Olga stopped at the end of the alley, turning to show William and Matilda they should do the same. At least she still had her wits.

William reached the end and peered in the army's direction. Sixty to seventy soldiers, Artan, Hawk, and Max among them as their prisoners. Six to eight drones hovered over the pack. They'd gathered in front of a large building. It looked like it had been used in the past to host sporting events. Where one of the shops had a large donut on the roof, this one wore the trophy of a man dressed in a helmet and padded gear. He had a stick, which he pressed into the ground. The front, a large steel windowless framework, led to some kind of indoor arena.

As the army filed into the building, the drones left them.

"They're heading this way." Matilda tugged on the back of William's shirt as she retreated.

"Are you sure?" Olga said.

No time for debate. Matilda ran back to the window leading into the shop on their right and dived through. William followed her a second later, Olga scrambling in on his heels.

All of them sat with their backs to the wall beneath the window. Less than a minute later, the brilliant white light from a drone flooded into the abandoned space, casting a bright glow across the dusty floor.

William raised his eyebrows at Matilda, who returned a tight-lipped smile.

The hum of the drone faded into the distance, and Olga said, "How did you know they'd come this way?"

"A hunch," Matilda said. "Maybe they're used to being followed. Maybe they're looking for more of Fury's army."

"So what do we do now?" Olga said. "There are a lot of soldiers in that arena."

William said, "I have an idea."

"Which is?"

"Follow me." William's body still protested his movements from where he'd fallen down the stairs while running through the towers, his shins buzzing, bruised from top to bottom. But there were greater needs than his suffering in that moment. He climbed back out into the alley.

CHAPTER 27

Max had seen Olga, but he couldn't tell the others. Hawk and Artan were too far away from him, and there were too many soldiers around for him to yell. Besides, Olga might have seen them, but the responsibility for getting out of this mess rested firmly on their shoulders. Hoping for Olga's help had to be plan B.

The army had taken Hawk's and Artan's knives. They'd frisked Max, but found nothing. Sixty to eighty soldiers, every one of them stared at Max and his friends, pressing in around them. They dared them to try something stupid. They only needed the slightest excuse.

"Move faster." A soldier shoved Max in the back. He stumbled into another one directly in front of him, who spun around, his baton raised.

Keeping his hands down, Max cowered away from the expected blow and kept his attention on the ground.

The soldier tutted and shook his head.

They were heading towards an arena. It had a giant statue of a man on the roof. The man leaned over a stick that looked more like a broom than anything you could play sport with. A steel framework dominated the front of the building. It had lost its glass a long time ago. It left the building exposed to the elements.

The lead soldiers entered the arena ahead of them, their brisk march echoing in the vast foyer. Dirty tiles covered the floor, much like the ones in the mall. Cracks ran through many of them. Memories of what this place had once been surrounded them. Small kiosks on either side, they housed broken machines with faded labels.

Something changed the sound of the army's steps. Max walked on tiptoes to peer over the heads of those in front of him. The foyer funnelled them into a tight corridor, forcing them to walk no more than five or six abreast. The bottleneck slowed the army, and those on either side of Max pressed against him in preparation for the tight passage.

Hawk and Artan walked into the corridor before Max. Small patches of paint clung to the walls and ceiling. The hallway had once been blue. It wouldn't be long before that memory peeled away, several more flakes falling like autumn leaves at the army's passing.

Max heaved when he stepped out of the other side of the corridor. Despite the high ceiling, the vinegar reek of rot filled the place. It hung heavy like humidity and curdled the air. It gagged him with its pungent and tangible funk. The diseased screams and roars quickened his pulse. He gulped, but it offered little relief.

Mad Max.

He shook his head.

Mad Max.

"No!"

A soldier on Max's right smirked and barged into him. "You're fucked!"

If only he knew. Maybe this would finally bring an end to the torment.

Mad Max.

The soldiers spread out when they exited the corridor. Their parting revealed the room's centrepiece. The sporting arena, rectangular with rounded corners. About two hundred feet long and a hundred feet wide, it had a wall running around its perimeter. The first four feet of the wall had been made from brick, the next six feet from glass or some other transparent material. It revealed the dense press of diseased contained within. Surely glass would have shattered by now.

A wooden platform with stairs leading to it sat level with the top of the wall. A plank protruded out over the sea of snapping and snarling fury.

Mad Max.

"Shut up!" Max knocked his head with his fist. The soldier on his left raised an eyebrow at him before he shot a derisive snort through his nose.

Artan already on the platform, Hawk climbed the stairs next.

The army occupied the spectators' area on the other side of the platform. The best seats in the house. Like in the stadium they'd run through with Gracie, the seats were made from plastic. Bleached blue plastic. They started ringside and ran all the way to the back wall, each row getting higher the farther back they went. The rows of seats encircled the ring and ran beneath the platform they currently stood on.

The presence of so many people riled the diseased. Their cries grew louder. They slammed open palms against the clear wall. Some of them pressed their faces against it, pus and blood coating the transparent barrier as they tried to bite through.

Mad Max.

A shove in the back encouraged Max up the stairs to join Artan and Hawk. The diseased grew more frantic. How many of the creatures had once been Fear's victims? How many diseased had they started with when they built this place?

The diseased and every soldier in the place watched Max and his friends. His heart slammed through him. Artan stood serene, as if he had a plan. Hawk twitched, his hands balled. He looked from side to side. Would he try to be a hero again?

Mad Max.

Even now, separated from a lot of Fear's army, there were still too many soldiers on the platform for Max to tell Artan and Hawk he'd seen Olga. But unless she came in now with something to rival this army, they were on their own anyway.

The soldiers mirrored the diseased. They banged against the clear wall like they wanted in.

Hawk's upper body twitched. What did he think he could do in this situation?

Mad Max.

Many of the rancid creatures wore the marks of how they'd been turned. Teeth marks on their faces and necks. Some of them were deep red and glistening with blood. Some wounds had turned black with age.

Mad Max.

Max twitched.

Mad Max.

About two hundred diseased in the ring. Max trembled and backed into the line of soldiers behind him. They shoved him forwards. Cyrus stared at him from the centre of the crowd. Cyrus. His brothers. His mum and dad. Hugh. Their maws snapped; they reached out to him with atrophied arms and twisted faces.

Mad Max.

Caved-in heads, bleeding eyes, yells of agony. Broken, they wanted this to end. But they wanted him more.

Mad Max.

Max balled his fists. If he ended up in there, could he beat every one of them to death? Could he protect his friends?

Mad Max.

A door in the wall opposite. Their way out? It must have been how the people who played the sport got into the arena. Surely it had been sealed shut a long time ago. The door handle had been removed. Maybe that was all they'd needed to do to keep it shut. The diseased didn't exactly have the best dexterity.

The gurning and grinning faces of the blue army surrounded the arena. Frenzied, the line between them and their foetid counterparts blurred. The chant started low and grew in volume. "Walk the plank! Walk the plank! Walk the plank!"

Max's saliva turned into a thick paste, his throat arid. His heart beat in his neck. He gulped and leaned close to Hawk. At least if he told him about Olga … but a soldier threw him a hard glare. He recoiled from the man's fury. If Olga had any intention of getting them out of there, she'd best arrive soon.

Five soldiers stood on the platform with Max and his friends. One of them held a long and curved sword. She used it to slice through the air. The spectators fell silent. The diseased weren't as compliant. They moaned and roared. They pawed at the transparent wall with clumsy slaps.

"Ladies and gentlemen," she said, her face red with the effort of shouting over the chaos. She had brown greasy hair slicked back in a ponytail, and her two front teeth were missing. It dragged a lisp across her words. She used her knife as she gesticulated along with her grandiose speech. "These people thought it was okay to walk through *our* city."

Gasps ran around the room. Many of the soldiers booed. Some of them shook their heads. Others hammered against the glass.

"I know," the knife-wielding woman said. "The cheek of it, right? Maybe they didn't realise this city belongs to us. I mean, the place is a wreck, and if they'd spoken to Fury, they'd be forgiven for assuming it was no more than a fighting arena for the two armies. But unlike Fury, we have ambition for this city beyond a no-man's-land." She stamped on the wooden platform when she said it. The crowd cheered. "We're taking this city back. We're putting more resources and more people into claiming this territory. First, we'll occupy the city, and then we'll take Fury. We'll move out like a plague, overrun them, and end this cursed war." The crowd cheered. "No longer will we send our kids to the slaughter in a fight with no purpose. Unlike Fury, we care about our citizens. We owe it to them to make this last push. This city is ours. Now we need to make sure the world knows it. So I say it's a good job we found these trespassers. They need to learn. They need to …" The woman cupped a hand to her ear.

The chaos of the crowd's screams and jeers melded into one singular chant. "Walk. The. Plank! Walk. The. Plank!"

The greasy woman smiled. Like before, she cut the air with her sword, commanding silence. The diseased continued to wail with discontent. They continued to shove one another and snarl. "But first," the woman said, "we decide who lives. Someone needs to tell the tale, right? To let everyone know this city belongs to Fear. A well-told story can repel would-be attackers as effectively as any army."

A soldier shoved Max, and he stumbled forwards another step. He stood in between Hawk and Artan. The three of them lined up facing the soldiers on the other side of the arena.

"So," the woman said, pointing at her three new prisoners with the tip of her sword, "which one do we save?" Max first, she levelled her blade on him. "This one?" A small section of the crowd cheered.

When the woman highlighted the scowling Hawk, the soldiers fell silent. If Hawk cared, he hid it well. He'd fight every one of them given half a chance, and he had no problem showing it.

And finally, Artan. His boyish good looks and tanned skin sent the crowd wild. Strong featured, brooding, and physically fit. Many of them slammed their open palms against the clear wall surrounding the rink. It shook and rattled. Many more stamped their feet. Whistles ran so shrill they forced Max's shoulders into his neck.

The woman with the sword grinned. She cut the air with her blade again. "Well, it looks like we have a clear favourite, then." Somewhere between a smile and a sneer lifted one side of her mouth when she looked Artan up and down. "It's just a shame we have to let him go. I could do with a new pet."

All the soldiers had entered the arena. And still no sign of Olga. Max needed to stall for time. Give her as long as he could. What other choice did they have? He opened his mouth, but someone cut him short.

"Val!" The call echoed in the tight corridor leading from the foyer to the arena.

The woman with the sword paused, and the crowd quietened.

Several soldiers entered. A scuffle amongst them. At first it looked like the blue army were fighting one another until a flash of red revealed the twisting and writhing form in their midst. Smaller than her captors, she continued to twist and turn as if it she could affect her current situation.

"Well, well." The woman with the knife smiled, stepping aside to avoid the flurry of activity being dragged up to the platform.

The soldiers with Max, Artan, and Hawk also moved

aside. Blood ran from the red soldier's nose. It coated the lower half of her face as a mask of blood. Swelling closed her right eye, and the other one remained open with just a squint.

The woman with the sword showed where she wanted Fury's soldier: in front of Max and his friends. A finer prize than the three boys. It bought Olga more time.

The soldiers' boos and jeers damn near shook the building's foundations.

This time, the woman with the knife basked in the chaos. She smiled and spread her arms wide. She then gestured at the two soldiers on the platform with her.

The back of Max's knees weakened when they kicked Fury's soldier at the same time. Her arms and legs flailed as if she could somehow find purchase in the air. A desperate and instinctive attempt to save a life already lost.

The diseased caught the red soldier's stage dive and dragged her under, burying her beneath a writhing and ravenous carpet.

The enclosed space amplified the soldiers' cheers, and Max's ears rang from their response. If he didn't take his moment now, he might not get another chance. He leaned close to his friends. "We might still get out of this."

"How do you work that out?" Hawk said.

The soldiers on the platform were occupied with their enemy's demise. "I saw Olga on the roof of a building. She watched us get caught. Hopefully, she'll work out a way to get us out of here."

"If she does," Artan said, "she'd best hurry the fuck up."

Max nodded, and his frame sagged. "Yeah." Who was he kidding? Olga and the others had no chance of saving them.

CHAPTER 28

William still hadn't explained his plan.

"William, what the hell are we doing back here?" Olga said.

As they approached the large building they'd seen the scavengers sleeping in earlier, William said, "There's, what, four hundred of them in there?"

The short girl shrugged. "'Bout that."

"And how many of Fear's soldiers did we see?"

"Eighty at the most."

"We saw what they did to that soldier who was strung up. So all we need to do—"

Olga finished the sentence for him. "Is bring them together."

"Right."

"I'm worried," Matilda said.

"Me too." William raised his index finger on his right hand. "But one thing I know for sure is we don't have the luxury of time. Who knows what they have planned for the others. They might already be doing whatever it is. So we need to make a decision. Are you both with me?"

Matilda nodded first before Olga shrugged. "Fine, let's do this. How are we going to get them to chase us?"

"We need to bait them."

"How?"

"Just be ready to run, okay?"

"Oh." Olga shook her head. "I don't like this one bit."

A pair of double doors dominated the front of the warehouse. They hung slightly ajar. When they'd peered in last, they'd only seen the first floor. Who knew how many more were hidden from sight on the level below. No matter how William tried to control his breathing as he closed in on the building, his heart still beat like it would burst, and his lungs were tight. Hopefully not so tight that he couldn't outrun the lot of them. He bit down on his bottom lip and pulled the left of the two doors wide. Just wide enough to allow him to slip into the large space.

Windows along two of the four walls let in enough light to show him no one slept on the ground floor. While they were large enough to show him the way, they were too small to encourage a breeze through the place. The reek of dirt, the result of so many unwashed bodies in an enclosed space, caught in the back of his throat. Dirt mixed with the funk of sweat from where the day heated up and slowly stewed the rancid scavengers.

The stairs leading to the first floor reminded William of every fire escape he'd climbed in this city. If it ain't broke … Metal, they led a zigzag from the ground, bending twice as they worked their way up the back wall.

As a kid, William and Matilda used to play a game called *What's the Time, Mr. Wolf?* A simple premise, one kid would be the wolf and stand with their back to the rest. They'd try to get the other kids to come as close to them as possible before they decided it was dinner time, turned around, and chased them. The kids would run off screaming, doing their best to avoid capture. At what point would the scavengers call dinner time?

William's legs shook when he reached the bottom of the stairs. A tight grip on the handrail, he took slow and deliberate steps to the first floor.

What's the time, Mr. Wolf?

He threw a glance back at the double doors, plotting his exit. Matilda directly behind him, Olga behind her. They both nodded. They were ready. Time to commit to the plan.

Heavy stamps up the final few stairs, William poked his head up into the first floor and clapped his hand to his mouth. "Oh, shit!" Half of the room were already awake. He said it loud enough to make sure he roused the other half. "Uh … I—"

Olga and Matilda ran.

A flash of white light crashed into William's vision, and fire ran through his sinuses. A scavenger had blindsided him and kicked him in the face. His sight blurred, he rolled back on his heels, grabbed for the railing at his side, and missed. The back of his head struck a lower step, the entire staircase ringing like a misshapen bell. His skull held the note as he came to a halt at the bottom.

He lay on his back on the concrete, his head throbbing, his sinuses stinging. A stream of scavengers descended the stairs, their footsteps playing a thunderous roar.

Back on his feet, his legs wobbly, his nose clogged with blood, William ran. More light flooded into the place when Olga kicked the door wide, Matilda following her out.

But the light vanished when the doors slammed shut. The closing lock rang through the room with a definitive *clunk!*

"What the …?" Alone in the warehouse, the scavengers charging down the metal stairs. William ground to a halt in front of the closed doors and turned to face the descending wave of fury. "Shit!"

CHAPTER 29

A complex pulley system ran along the ceiling from the bottom of the stairs to the double doors. It gave the scavengers total control over who entered and who left.

William ran for the wall on his right. The windows were only four feet wide by two feet deep. They were at least six feet from the ground. He dived as if about to enter water, his hands stretched out in front of him. But he hadn't jumped high enough. He landed on his stomach across the wall. He kicked his legs, catching a scavenger with the backswing of his right boot as he wriggled through. He landed headfirst in the alley to another flash of white light.

"What happened?" Matilda said the second William charged out into the main road.

He shook his head. "Don't worry about it. Just run!"

Overtaking both Olga and Matilda, the two girls paused for the briefest of moments until the *crash* of the warehouse's front doors swung open. The scavengers spilled from the large building like a plague. Their thunderous, collective roar damn near shook the ground. They were the most lucid and focused horde they'd encountered. No chance of avoiding this lot by climbing on a roof and hiding from sight.

The kick to the face and fall down the stairs had left William's nose clogged with blood. He breathed through his mouth. They only had to get to the arena. They could do this.

The front of the arena was wide open. It showed William the smaller corridor inside, the mass of blue soldiers beyond that. Get the scavengers and Fear's army together, and surely they'd do the rest.

The scavengers had closed the gap, some front-runners eating away at the distance between them, but they weren't close enough. Olga on one side, Matilda on the other, William ran into the arena's foyer and threw his arms wide. "Come on, then, you fucks!"

The blue soldiers turned as one. Frowns of confusion morphed into scowling rage. But none of them charged.

"What are they waiting for?" Matilda said.

A woman appeared in the corridor. She had greasy brown hair, and her two front teeth were missing. She carried a long curved sword. Many of the soldiers behind her held batons.

The scavengers had halted outside the arena. The group at least three to four hundred strong, they stood waiting, many of them panting from the run.

"Well, well," the woman said, her words wet with a lisp from her lack of front teeth. "This is a pleasant surprise. You went to the effort of delivering yourselves to us." The woman waved at the pack of scavengers and said, "Thank you."

One of the group stepped forward and nodded. "You'll leave us something?"

The blue soldiers had followed their leader into the foyer. They surrounded William, Olga, and Matilda, patting them down for weapons.

The soldier frisking Matilda took it too far, and William lurched in his direction. "What the fuck are you doing?"

Another flash of white light, the soldier punched him square on the nose. William dropped to his knees and held his face in his hands.

A female soldier, about five feet tall, kicked William in the stomach and spat on him. "Now get up, you pathetic fuck."

Before anyone else could weigh in, William stumbled to his feet, his stomach tied in a knot of nausea. He shook, and blood rained down the back of his throat.

"What?" the woman with the knife said. "You thought you could turn the scavengers against us? They're the only people we allow to live in our city. They clean up our mess. We have a symbiotic relationship with them. And we know to stay the fuck away from one another." The pack of scavengers were already rounding the corner back towards their warehouse, but the lead woman spoke in a mock whisper anyway. "They don't know this yet, but when we get control back of this city, we will drive them away from here like rats from a burning ship. But until then, we're—" she paused, tapping her chin as if it helped her think "—associates." Her laugh bubbled from deep within her throat and she shook her head. "I can't believe you wanted to use them against us. O'well, I suppose we should give you what you wanted, eh? I mean, this was about reuniting you with your friends, right?"

As they led the three of them away, William dropped his attention to the dirty and broken tiles at his feet. What an idiot. It had seemed like a good plan.

CHAPTER 30

Mad Max.

Max shook his head, the diseased's call like a mosquito buzzing inside his skull.

There had been five soldiers on the platform with them before, but now, as Val brought William, Olga, and Matilda up to join them, she also brought seven more of her blue-uniformed friends. Max and Olga stared at one another. How the fuck had they both ended up here?

As she'd done before, Val cut the air with her sword, extinguishing the crowd's excitement. The diseased groaned and yelled in defiance of Fear's psychotic leader.

Mad Max.

Cyrus stared up from the crowd. His mum and dad. His brothers. William … he did a double take. Not William. William stood behind him, close to Matilda and Artan.

"So," Val said, "it would seem our prisoners have some friends." She laughed. "Friends that were stupid enough to think they could use the scavengers as a weapon against us."

Mad Max.

The plank led away from the platform out over the diseased. A sea of twitching fury. They had but one purpose: to drive this vile plague into clean blood. The dense press of the crowd would make it damn near almost impossible to move when they ended up down there. How on earth would Max protect his friends?

Fury's soldier had now become part of the collective mess. She stared up through eyes that matched her uniform. Her arms were pinned to her sides from the tight press of bodies. Deprived of reaching towards the platform, she bit at the air like a dog bothered by a fly. Her head snapped one way and then the other.

"Of course," Val said, "we're going to leave one of them as a symbol of friendship for the scavengers. A live meal, we might even leave them unharmed." She tapped her chin, her fingernails broken and dirty. "But which one?"

Many of the crowd shouted. Among the general noise, Max heard, "The short one." His stomach clamped.

Mad Max.

Until now, Max hadn't noticed the large pole on one corner of the platform. Too much else to focus on. It had looked like a part of the structure. But it offered nothing to the integrity of their improvised stage, and it had ropes tied around it. What did they use it for?

Milking the crowd, Val used her sword to point to William first. "This one?"

The crowd made some noise, but they'd proved they could do better when they'd cheered for Artan.

Then onto Matilda. "This one?"

Val had heard the calls for the small one. How could she not? Did that reflect the nature of their relationship with the scavengers? They'd leave them someone to feed on, but it would be the slimmest pickings of the lot. After all, they were a pack of cannibals. And why would Fear pass up the chance to give them a reminder of their role in their relationship? They'd take what they were given and be grateful.

Val pointed the tip of her sword at Olga. The crowd noise trebled, the closed roof amplifying their joy. It made Max's ears ring and buried Val's words. Not that it mattered what she said. They'd chosen Olga.

Val nodded at two soldiers on the platform with her. The hairs on the back of Max's arms rose as if the air held a charge. They didn't know Olga like he did.

The first one grabbed Olga's right arm while the second tried to grab her left. But Olga moved fast, catching the second one with a wild hook that sent him stumbling backwards.

Were it not for Val catching the soldier by his lapels, he would have fallen into the pit. The near miss silenced the raucous crowd and invigorated the creatures below.

Val turned the soldier around so he faced the crowd on the other side. "This, ladies and gentlemen, is an example of what not to do. Lower your guard in this city and you're screwed. She can't be any taller than five feet—"

"Five feet two!" Olga said through clenched teeth, the first soldier still clinging onto her.

"Well, there we have it." Val winked at Olga. "I do apologise, sweetheart. Five feet two." She spun the soldier around, her tone deepening. Her words damn near crackled. "You let a girl of no more than five feet get the better of you." She shoved the soldier backwards from the platform. He screamed as he went down. He fixed on Val while the diseased caught him and dragged him under.

Mad Max.

Her face puce, Val's sword shook as an extension of her arm when she pointed down at the spot where the soldier had been. "I will *not* stand for that level of incompetence."

She spun around, her blade making a *whoosh* as it cut through the air. "You!"

A woman in blue pointed at herself as if she really didn't want it to be her.

"Tie her up," Val said.

Olga's left hand still free, the woman led with a punch, catching Olga hard enough to stun her. She then grabbed Olga's left arm before helping the other guard tie her to the pole. They'd leave her there for now. Their offering to the scavengers.

"Now—"

In one move, Max snatched the sword from Val's hand, ran the length of the plank, and jumped into the diseased crowd.

CHAPTER 31

While everyone watched Max, William clenched his jaw and kicked Val in the back. Her feet lifted clean off the platform, and she swan-dived into the diseased. One creature drew blood from her shoulder before she vanished from sight. Her scream died as she drowned beneath the writhing fury.

Matilda shoved one soldier and then another from the platform and untied Olga while Hawk took the fight to three more.

Artan, like his sister, opted to clear the platform, ending Hawk's fight with the three soldiers as soon as it had begun. He shoved two over the side and kicked a third into the pit with the creatures.

More of Fear's army climbed the platform's stairs, their batons raised. But the narrow path inhibited their attack, presenting them to the now liberated Olga in a line that made them easy to repel. She yelled as she kicked them away, sending them back into the crowd around the bottom of the stairs.

A soldier waved his baton at her. "You have to come down

at some point."

Now they had control of the platform, Olga and Hawk ready for any attack, William turned to Max. He shoved and barged his way through the diseased crowd.

Many of the soldiers in the spectator area nudged one another and pointed. They had no idea what was coming their way.

Val's sword in his hand, Max fell against the clear top section of the wall. The slap of his open palm sent several of the soldiers back a pace. He'd reached what had once been a door that must have provided access to the ring. The handles had long since been removed.

"Ah," William said. And even with chaos around them, he smiled.

The gap around the edge of the door wide enough for Max to slide the blade through, he drove more blue soldiers away when he thrust the sword at them and dragged it down the gap to where the latch kept the door shut. The sword slid straight through and the door opened. He shoved it wide into the space the army had just cleared.

At the head of the charge, Max led the diseased from the rink. His sword out in front of him, he slashed at the soldiers. Many of the crowd had already taken off, heading in the foyer's direction. But those at the front fell, and they fell fast.

The diseased spread out, attacking anyone close to them. Anyone, save Max.

Screams and cries spread through the crowd. Those behind William at the bottom of the stairs, those still trying to do their duty by getting to their prisoners on the platform, were yet to get the message.

William shouted over the chaos, "Artan, Matilda." They turned his way, the familial resemblance as clear now as ever.

"We're going to have a small window to get away from here before every soldier in this place is infected. You need to be ready to run." And then to Hawk and Olga, his throat sore from shouting, "Did you hear me?"

"Yep!" Olga called back, her features set, her teeth bared as she kicked another soldier down the stairs.

"Hawk?"

William shared a look with Olga. "No more heroics, okay? The second we get the chance, we run. We'll probably get split up, but we know where the meeting point is. You hear me, Hawk?"

The wildfire panic had reached the soldiers on their side. Many of them had already run. Hawk turned William's way and nodded. "Okay. But I'm worried we won't all make it."

"Just worry about you. It's every man and woman for themselves until we get to the tower."

The space at the bottom of the stairs cleared. "On my count," William said.

"Three …"

"Two …"

"One."

The five of them moved in single file, Hawk in the lead. He descended the stairs two at a time and broke away at the bottom.

They should have planned it better.

Olga and Hawk joined the blue army's mass exodus to their right.

Matilda and Artan went straight ahead, climbing the spectators' seating.

William went left.

Too late now. They each had to take their own path. Hopefully, they'd all find their way to the tower.

CHAPTER 32

Nothing William could do about it now. They'd agreed they'd find their separate ways out of there, and he needed to stick to that. Many of the soldiers ran for the exit, but the narrow tunnel created an impossible bottleneck, and the diseased had already caught up to the mass exodus. They chewed into the congestion with snarling ferocity. He headed for the opposite end of the arena.

The spectators' area on this side was a mirror image of the one Fear's soldiers gathered on to watch them walk the plank. Rows of seats, they lifted in steps, growing progressively higher the farther they were from the ring. They ran all the way to the wall. While avoiding Fear's soldiers, William climbed.

Sweat itched William's collar, his brow damp by the time he reached the top row of seats and closed in on the arena's far wall.

Screams and shouts filled the air as Fear's army fell to the diseased attack. Those soldiers at the front had tried to flee while those at the back waded in to help their brethren. They were all failing.

A wide rectangular window only two feet tall ran the width of the arena's back wall. As absent of glass as almost every other window in this city, the breeze cooled William's sweating skin. The frenzied crowd by the narrow corridor turned gradually more chaotic, the diseased tearing through them, overpowering them. Their cries for help morphed into wails of insanity. Maybe, in the heat of battle, each soldier thought they had a chance. Would they still think that if they were watching it all unfold from his vantage point?

William's stomach lurched when he poked his head outside. The wind cooled his sweating face. A series of metal cables ran from the side of the building to the ground like guy ropes. Several of them started just below the window ledge. A way down, but if he screwed this up, he had a thirty-foot fall onto concrete. The snarls and shrill screams behind him turned up a notch. Risking the fall had to be better than any other option.

The yell of a soldier nearby. William pulled back inside and spun around. The man brandished a baton, his teeth clenched as he bore down on him.

Weaponless, William raised his fists.

The soldier stepped over the seats with long strides.

William widened his stance.

The soldier yelled as he jumped the last seat in his path, caught both feet on the bleached plastic, and fell. His head crashed into the wall with a *tonk*. His eyes rolled back. His body fell limp.

The soldier lay unconscious, his face pressed against the concrete step. William pried his baton from his tight grip and slid it down the back of his trousers so his belt held it in place. The arena, a writhing hive of chaos, his friends still nowhere to be seen. He climbed out of the window and hung from the ledge with both hands.

William's clothes flapped in the wind, and his grip ached.

The shrill cries were muted now he'd climbed outside. Rust coated the metal cables, but they remained taut as if they played a part in keeping the arena standing. Freckled with corrosion, the rough rust cut into William's hands when he reached down. "This is going to hurt."

William let go of the window ledge and caught the cable with his other hand. He clung on, his body falling into a pendulous swing.

Hand over hand, William made his way down the cable's forty-five-degree angle. Thankfully, he had enough purchase to avoid sliding. The rough steel would have sheared his palms off. His knuckles aching, he progressed by a foot at a time on his slow descent towards the ground.

With the drop reduced to about six feet, William let go, the shock of landing snapping through him. One last check for Matilda and the others. He shook his head and took off into the city, the arena at his back. He'd get away from this place first, and then he'd find his way to Gracie's tower. Hopefully the others would do the same.

CHAPTER 33

William had gone the long way around to avoid the chaos spilling from the arena. It had taken him a few hours, any trace of dawn burned away by the bright sun. Leaning against the large discoloured donut, he squinted and shielded his eyes to give him a better view of the tower below.

As good a place to rest as any, he'd watched the door in the tower's base for the past fifteen minutes. No one had gone in or out. Were his friends already inside?

On the ground, a main road separated William from the tower. Still no soldiers, red or blue. And, more importantly, no dogs or drones.

While gripping onto the baton he'd taken from Fear's soldier, William burst from cover and sprinted across the road. Exposed in broad daylight, he ran with his back hunched like being a few inches lower would make a difference.

The door's hinges creaked when William opened it. The faces of his friends squinted against the glare. Hawk held a baton in preparation for a fight.

William slipped in and closed the door behind him, throwing the place back into darkness. Max, Olga, and Hawk were in the tower. Max's face was covered in blood, his hair matted and glistening. The stench of disease caught on the back of William's throat. He coughed and gulped against the gagging itch. "Where are they?" The short run hadn't been enough to make him breathless, but he panted anyway, his chest tight. He asked again, his voice higher in pitch, "Where are they?"

Olga replied in a sombre tone, "They're not here yet. We hoped you might have them with you."

"Shit." Something else lay beneath Olga's delivery. The slightest hint of an apology. "You've held up four fingers to the camera, haven't you?"

"It's been a couple of hours since we left the arena. Can you blame us?"

"You could—"

"How long did you expect us to wait? How long is too long?"

"So you're ready to trust Gracie now?" William said. "Now it means saving your arse."

Olga sighed. "Really, William? After all we've been through. Besides, is there another option that's going to get us out of here? We're tired."

"And I'm not?"

"I didn't say that."

"Look." Max spoke this time. "We decided together. We've waited."

"Not long enough."

"Come on, William," Max said, "we're going around in circles now."

Olga said, "We *all* need to rest and get cleaned up."

William shrugged, for what good it did in the darkness. Max had been to hell and back. He'd not been himself for weeks now. He'd earned the right to rest. "I'm not going with you. Not until I've found Matilda and Artan. I'd rather die than leave them behind."

Light flooded into the space. William spun in the door's direction, mirroring Hawk as he readied his baton.

"Gracie," Max said. His voice cracked from where he clearly struggled to hold onto his emotions. "Thank you for coming."

The red-headed girl dipped a stoic nod, slipped into the room, and closed the door behind her. "Where are Artan and Matilda?"

"We don't know," William said.

"But Olga signalled for me to come and get you. We never come into the city in the daylight. That's the rules. Are you now telling me you're not ready to leave?"

"No." Olga's firm voice whipped around the enclosed space. "I'm ready to go, and I'm pretty sure Hawk and Max are too."

When neither of the boys argued, William's heart sank. His voice weak, he said, "I'm not. I can't give up hope on Matilda and Artan. If that means you won't come back and we're on our own after this, then so be it."

A soft hand rested against William's forearm, and Gracie spoke gentle words. "I *will* come back, but not in daylight again."

"At least that gives me the entire day. Better to have a bit too much time than not enough."

"Okay," Gracie said. "We'll monitor the camera for your return. The same thing applies. When you're ready for me to come and get you, hold up four fingers on your right hand. Unless I see you waiting with Matilda and Artan."

"You *will* see me with them."

"I hope so. Right, let's get the hell out of here before I regret my decision to come out while it's light."

Dazzled again by the sun's glare, William blinked while his friends followed Gracie, and then joined them in leaving the tower. There seemed little point in waiting alone in the dark. If Matilda and Artan hadn't made it to the tower by now, the chances were they needed his help.

CHAPTER 34

Where else for William to go but back to the arena? He'd travelled the relatively safe route across the rooftops and now stood several hundred feet from the enormous structure. An open patch of concrete separated him from the sporting venue. A spot where fans would have gathered on match day, waiting for the big event. But instead of fans, over one hundred diseased congregated in the space. They snarled and snapped, hissed and spat. They slammed into one another with their aimless wanderings. Many of them were dressed in Fear's blue uniforms. The pity that usually twisted through his stomach to witness the wretched degradation of a human being was remarkably absent for those dressed in blue. The matching clothes highlighted the uniformity of their purpose. A hive mind with just one goal. The disease drove them. Slaves to it, they existed to ensure it thrived.

But no sign of Matilda and Artan. Unless …

Five drones hovered around the corner of the large arena like wasps around a rotting apple. They swerved and twisted, bobbed and weaved. They were waiting for something. But what?

Matilda and Artan had to still be alive. They were survivors. If he'd gotten away from this in one piece, surely they had too. The mid-morning sun glistened on the scrapes and dents in the arena's steel roof from where the drones had shot at the building. But they were still there, so they couldn't have caught their prey. Something held the drones' attention. Whatever it was, he had to investigate.

Although, how on earth would he get past the creatures between him and the arena?

∼

WILLIAM CROSSED over the roofs from one building to the next. He shouldn't get his hopes up, but it had to be them. Who else would hide so close to the arena? Whoever it was, they were an enemy of the blue army; otherwise the drones would have left them alone. The white gravel crunched beneath his steps. Some small stones sprayed up when he skidded to a halt on the roof of the building next to the scavengers' warehouse.

Dropping onto his front, William crawled along the gravel and peered over the edge. They'd tied the double doors shut with chains and a chunky padlock. Had they abandoned the place?

Tock!

A scavenger climbed out of a first-floor window onto the metal walkway attached to the side of the building. William drew his baton. He lay flatter than before, the small white stones digging into his chin.

The scavenger, a man with long, greasy, unkempt hair, walked with stooped shoulders and barked a phlegmy cough.

William's heart slammed against the rough roof.

But the man had come out to check on the diseased. After leaning away from the building to peer down the street, he shook his head, sighed and returned to the window he'd only just climbed from.

William gave it a minute before he shuffled away from the warehouse, jumped back to his feet, and took off towards the arena for a second time.

Consistent with many of the small buildings in this section of the city, the one closest to the arena had a fire escape. Thankfully, it ran down the side farthest away from the diseased mob. He didn't need them watching him make his way towards them.

A handrail ran to the ground with the zigzagged stairs. At the bottom, he kicked a section. One side of it snapped free with a *clang!* Once he'd worked the other side free and liberated the three-foot steel bar, he headed towards the arena and the diseased crowd.

The soldier's baton tucked down the back of his trousers and the handrail in a two-handed grip, William's palms sweated and his heart thumped. He swallowed against the dry itch in his throat. The plan had been easier to make when he'd been twenty feet higher than the creatures. Now he stood eyeball to eyeball … But what other choice did he have?

The drones remained near the corner of the arena. Matilda and Artan would starve to death rather than give up. If Matilda and Artan were even inside the building.

If he thought about it for much longer, he'd change his mind. William stepped from the alleyway and coughed to clear his throat.

About twenty diseased turned his way. Forty bleeding eyes. Lips pulled back, rattling snarls, angry hissing. William ran. The diseased gave chase.

A lead of about thirty feet. Hopefully, it would be enough.

William led them away from the arena, the metal pole in his grip. Their clumsy steps beat a tattoo against the asphalt, some of them yelling and yipping as their balance failed and they went down.

Not far to run, but fear robbed the strength from William's legs. He focused on his destination. Whether they fell over or not, looking back wouldn't help his cause.

The large doors at the front of the scavengers' warehouse clattered when William slammed into them. The bar in his grip, he shook as he threaded it into the loop of the lock. He froze when he glanced to his right at the wall of diseased closing in.

William tugged against the lock, yelling as he pulled. "Yeargh!" It broke into several small pieces. The chains sloughed from their loops and fell to the ground with a splash. William pulled the doors wide and charged into the warehouse. A scavenger waited for him. Teeth bared, he hissed like a diseased.

William smashed the metal bar over the dirty man's head. One blow proved enough.

Before the scavengers could use their pulley system to close the doors, the diseased streamed into the building.

The bar in his grip, William ran towards the bottom of the stairs. Many of the scavengers retreated to the first floor, shouting to those above them. But several guarded the pulley, tugging the ropes in a futile attempt to defend their home.

Small windows in the walls on William's left and right. He charged at the scavengers on the pulley and dived through one like he'd done the last time he'd escaped the building. Except, this time, when he landed on the ground in the alley outside, the only thing following him were the screams of falling scavengers.

William ran from the alley on wobbly legs. Panic burst from the warehouse's windows. Throat-tearing cries.

Diseased snarls. Footsteps against metal as some of the scavengers climbed out to the fire escape on the first floor.

Armed with his steel pole, William headed back towards the arena. He used the main road that ran parallel to the one he'd led the diseased down. He tracked his progress with the fire escapes along his side of the buildings until he came to the one with the missing railing. He cut into the alley he'd already run down and halted at the end. A quick check. The diseased had gone. Some were gathered by the scavengers' warehouse, but many of them were already inside. And good riddance. The scavengers' behaviour made them subhuman. Worse than the diseased. Fuck them.

There wouldn't be a better chance. William ran from the alley for a second time. But now he headed towards the arena.

The drones remained focused on the arena's roof as if nothing had changed. As if the diseased were invisible to them. William ran towards them with light steps. They were yet to turn his way. The arena, like the hotel he'd led the drones into, had an underground carpark. The best place to handicap the vicious killing machines.

"Best make this count," William muttered to himself. Fifteen feet from the drones, he pulled the soldier's baton from the back of his trousers and yelled, "Tilly! Artan!"

Five spotlights turned his way. Even in the daytime, their combined glare dazzled him. He launched the baton, drawing the machine's fire.

"William?"

The whir of the drones' guns. Their spinning ends had turned into glowing red circles.

"Tilly?" William threw the steel pole. The drones shot at it.

"What are you doing?"

William ran. The drones' bullets ate into the asphalt

where he'd stood moments before. "Get to the tower. Gracie will meet us there after dark."

William zigzagged to make himself harder to shoot. He turned a sharp left down the ramp to the car park beneath the arena.

The acoustics of being underground made it sound like the number of drones' had doubled.

A steel door over to William's right. There might be better options, but if the drones turned their lights off, he'd be running blind. He ran through the door and slammed it shut behind him. The ting of bullet fire sprayed the other side.

"Fuck!" He'd expected a staircase. He'd found a small room. Filled with old plastic bottles and several ratty brooms, he'd run into the cleaner's cupboard. He grabbed a chair and wedged it beneath the door handle. That would only hold for so long.

The spray of bullet fire against the other side of the door started his countdown. At some point, the steel would yield to their assault. If William hadn't found a way out by then, their bullets would tear him to shreds.

CHAPTER 35

A steel door might have separated William from the drones, but there were steel doors and there were steel doors. This one had already started to yield to the first spray of bullets. A splattering of indents evidenced their attack. The drones had to run out of ammo at some point, but he couldn't bank on that. And like with Matilda and Artan in the arena's roof, they could wait there forever for him to come out. He'd starve before they got bored.

Thud!

William jumped away from the door, crashing into a row of rusting metal shelves behind him. A drone had slammed into it, the impression of its contact pushing into the room. The glow from the drones' lights flooded through the new gaps both above and below.

Thud!

A second drone hit the door and bent it further. "Shit!" William muttered. How did he get himself stuck in a dark cleaning cupboard? Although, while dark, it wasn't pitch black. It hadn't been pitch black even before the bent door let in the drones' light. A weak glow came into the room from a vent up to his right where the wall met the ceiling.

Thud!

The door couldn't withstand this attack. The vent cover, between two to three feet square, fronted a metal tunnel of a similar size. Along with a faint glow of daylight, it ushered in the slightest breeze.

Thud!

Wherever it took him, anywhere had to be better than his current spot.

Hum-thud!

The longer the drones believed him to be cowering on the other side of the door, fearing his imminent end from their rotating guns, the more time he'd have to get out of there. If he could avoid giving the game away …

Reaching up, William gripped the vent cover and held his breath. The hum of another drone closed in.

Hummmmm-thud!

William tugged as the drone connected. The cover came free in his hands.

Thud!

The gap along the bottom of the door would soon be wide enough to give a drone access to the room. William trembled as he rested the liberated grate against the wall. He had the heartbeat of a panicked mouse, but he fought against it. Slow and steady. He needed to get away from there without them knowing. He pushed his arms into the tunnel and wriggled his upper body into the tight space after them.

Thud!

A tight metal crawlspace, he shuffled all the way in, an inch or two's clearance on either side of his body.

Thud!

The drones' attacks grew fainter as William crawled farther away. The tunnel changed direction up ahead, which blocked much of the light, but it didn't stop the fresh breeze. The smell of freedom ... If he moved fast enough.

Thud.

The tunnel took a vertical right-angled turn. William turned over onto his back, the echo of his own gasping breaths mocking him. It joined the sounds of his scrambling feet from where he kicked and scraped to turn himself over.

Thud. Thud.

The vertical section of the tunnel stretched up by about four feet. William slapped his hands against the tunnel's flat metal walls, bracing against the smooth sides, and sat up in the tight space. He turned and pulled his knees around, dragging them under him before he stood up. The short vertical section forced him to stoop. He faced down the tunnel at the brighter daylight at the end. The air fresher than before, it turned his sweating skin cool.

Thud.

William stretched forwards for a second time, reaching his hands out ahead of him towards daylight. He jumped and caught himself by slamming his feet against either side of the vertical tunnel. The metal cold against his chest, William slithered towards daylight, pulling himself with his upper body.

Thud!

The rending of steel was followed by the clatter of a falling door. An angry burst of gunfire tore into the room he'd left behind.

William pulled with his arms and then pushed with his feet. He moved down the tunnel like a frog swimming through mud, his panicked breaths echoing in the tight space. Focused on the exit, he pulled and then pushed, pulled and then pushed, pulle—

A hinged grate gave way beneath William, falling from

the bottom of the tunnel. It squeaked as it swung. It hung down into the dark car park.

He could jump down now and escape. He'd be quicker on foot. But it would also land him much closer to the drones, and he still couldn't see well.

The hum of the drones' engines echoed off the car park's walls.

William dragged his body over the grate and continued towards the light. Daylight would give him a better chance of survival.

Six feet from the grate leading outside, the hum of a drone's propellors grew so loud William halted. They were in the car park beneath him where the grate had swung open. The brilliant glow from its spotlight flooded the tunnel, reflecting off the shining metal. Had it seen him?

The drone's spinning guns whined.

A spray of bullets burst through the open hole. They ate into the steel air vent's roof.

The line of fire moved towards William, punching up through the part of the tunnel he'd just slid across.

William braced his feet against either side of the tunnel and pushed forwards. He pulled with his hands while the bullet fire behind him tore holes through the steel. If the thing stopped shooting for a moment, it might hear him.

As the drone ripped the ventilation shaft to shreds, William reached the grate at the end. He slammed an open palm against it. The metal cover fell away and clattered against the concrete outside.

Only a foot to the ground, William squirmed from the shaft as if birthed from it. He landed hard on his right shoulder, scrambled to his feet, and took off at a sprint in the direction of Gracie's tower.

CHAPTER 36

The deep rumble of an exploding mine called to them through the city. "That's what, the fifth one?" William said.

Artan's voice came from the darkness. "The seventh."

"Wow, that many? I suppose the city's probably dealing with more diseased in its streets than it's had in a long time." After escaping the drones, William followed what had become a familiar path back to Gracie's tower. Matilda and Artan were waiting for him.

"You know," William said, "I felt grateful for the chance to rest."

"For the first two hours," Matilda said.

"Right. Now it's getting tedious. How much longer do you think it will be until Gracie gets here?"

Artan's deep voice resonated in the enclosed space. "It must be dark out now."

The *clack* of the door handle snapped down. Groaning hinges ushered moonlight into the room.

While blinking, William stumbled to his feet and squinted at the silhouette. "Gracie?"

"Who else would it be?"

"I dunno. A lot's happened in this city I wasn't expecting."

Gracie walked over to Matilda, held her hand down, and pulled her to her feet. "So are you all ready to go?"

"How's it looking out there?" Artan said.

"There are a lot of diseased. The others told me how you broke out of the ice hockey arena. Fear's army is going to be gunning for you lot."

William shook his head. "We don't intend on coming back."

Gracie stepped towards the door. "I think that's a wise choice. Now let's go."

They headed away from the city, the ice hockey arena and metal tower at their backs.

After five minutes running, the buildings turned to rubble much like the house they'd camped in before entering the city. Ruin started at the edge of this place and ate its way in. It slowly chewed through the buildings like the disease slowly chewed through humanity. A rising tide of inevitability.

Gracie slowed the pace. There were too many obstacles waiting to trip them up if they were careless. Walls only a foot high, sheets and lumps of steel, metal bars encased and protruding from chunks of concrete. Their rusty fingers would tear skin and infect wounds.

A sheet of metal like many others in the ruins, Gracie checked around before she hunched down and dragged it clear, revealing a plain hatch. She pulled a key from her pocket and slid it into a hole that had been hard to spot at first. A gentle *clack,* she lifted the door to reveal a tunnel beneath. She slid in and moved aside to let the others follow.

After closing the hatch, Gracie flicked a switch on the wall. It lit the place up.

"Jeez!" William covered his burning eyes. "That's bright."

"It needs to be down here."

Despite its raggedy entrance, the square tunnel belonged to a different time. Smooth, dark grey steel panels on the floor, walls, and ceiling. Highly polished, they gave off a reflective shine, enhancing the glow from the lights.

~

It took them about ten minutes to reach another steel door, which Gracie knocked against seven times.

The *crack* of a bolt freed on the other side. The hinges groaned.

William's jaw fell wide as he followed Gracie into her community. The guard stood aside. In his early twenties, he had large features, a thick brow, jet black hair, and a jawline that could have been carved from rock. At least six feet five inches tall, he had thick hands and wide shoulders. He scowled in response to William's smile. Miserable bastard.

The tunnel had transitioned them from the past to the future. It had been both functional and unlike anything William had ever seen. And then they reached her community. William's jaw fell wide. "It's like we've entered a new world." Similar flooring to the tunnel, inasmuch as they had the floor, walls, and ceiling lined with steel, but there were many more lights. Although they gave off a duller glow, they revealed the intricate patterns on the walls. They showed them many doors leading to what must have been other parts of the complex.

"Welcome to Dout. This is where we live. It's late, so most people are sleeping. It's why we've dimmed the lights. Despite living underground, we try to follow the natural rhythm of day and night to keep everyone's sleep cycles regular. These"—she pointed at the light bulbs—"are UV bulbs."

"What does that mean?" Artan said.

"UV rays are important. It's what we get from the sun. These bulbs, while not a perfect substitute, emit the same rays, which help us stay healthy. Anyway"—she batted the air with her hand—"I'm sure you're tired and need to rest. Let me show you to where you're staying. The others are already in your room. I'll give you more of a tour of the place and introduce you to everyone tomorrow."

William's entire body had throbbed with a dull ache for hours, but now faced with the prospect of rest, his muscles twitched as if they might seize. Pains ran from the tips of his toes to the ends of every strand of hair. His heart flirted with a fatigue-induced panic attack, forcing him to take deep gulps. Standing aside so Gracie could lead them away, he let Artan and Matilda walk ahead of him. All the while, the watchful eyes of the guard who'd let them in burned into the back of his skull. But that was his job, right? To protect the community. And who wouldn't suspect new people?

A shake of his head to derail his spiralling thoughts, William fought against his urge to turn and face the guard, his back tingling at the imagined knife plunging into it. But they were supposed to be suspicious. He'd be the same. And for now, they needed to rest.

CHAPTER 37

The dim lights gradually brightened, easing William back to wakefulness. The second he'd lain down the previous evening, he'd passed out. Although, while his mind had rested, his body had a lot more healing to do. Before he'd fallen onto the soft mattress last night, he'd ached from head to toe. And, if anything, the rest had made it worse.

Someone knocked on the door. From the way the others instantly raised their heads, they'd been lying awake too. Max, Artan, Matilda, William, Olga, Hawk, and Dianna had all chosen to share a room despite being offered separate accommodation. They didn't know this place, and until they did, they were better together.

Olga spoke in a croaky voice. "Come in."

But the door remained closed, and the person knocked again.

Olga called louder this time. "Come in!"

Gracie replied, the closed door muffling her response, "You have to let me in."

Artan groaned as he got out of bed. The boy had stamina

and strength, but he hid it in his slim frame. Wiry, every bone in his body visible, he'd yet to reach the age where he'd changed from boy to man. Their sparse diet over the past few weeks hadn't helped.

Crack! Artan slammed his palm against the panel in the wall. The door slid open.

A slight flush to her pale skin, Gracie looked down before looking into Artan's eyes. She then focused anywhere but on the boy. William smiled and raised his eyebrows at Matilda.

"Uh …" Gracie said, "breakfast's ready." She turned her back on the room. "I'll wait outside for you to get changed."

Olga laughed. "You sure you don't want more of an eyeful?"

Gracie walked away.

∼

THE DINING HALL was a functional space. The same daylight bulbs lit the room, which had rows of benches and tables throughout to accommodate what appeared to be a large community. There were already at least two hundred people in the room. Every one of them watched William and the others enter the hall.

Olga spoke from the side of her mouth, loud enough for everyone to hear. "Well, this is awkward."

Gracie led them to one corner of the room. As he walked behind her, weaving through the tables, William's stomach rumbled and his mouth watered.

There were seven plates laden with food. William sat down and lifted a bread roll. Still warm, he tore it open, releasing a waft of steam. They each had a small bowl on their plate filled with strawberry jam. He spread a chunk on his roll and shoved the entire thing into his mouth.

Gracie smiled. "For a small community, we eat well."

"I can see that."

"Now enjoy." Smiling again, Gracie left them to eat.

～

For about ten minutes, they ate without talking to one another. Partly because of their hunger, partly because of their lack of privacy. They were still the most exciting thing to walk into the dining hall that morning. However, each of them tried to talk to the children who approached them. Wordless in their curiosity at the new people to enter their community, not a single one replied, and it didn't take long for a parent or guardian to come over, wince a silent apology, and drag their child back to their seat.

William smiled at Matilda. "It's nice to see some normal families again. To see kids being kids. I didn't realise just how much I've missed that."

Silence swept through the room. A monster of a man entered. Much like the guard on the gate the previous evening, but older. He also stood about six feet five inches tall. Broad shouldered, his dark black hair had flecks of grey running through it. He had large features and wore a deep scowl. The guard from the previous evening followed him in. They must have been father and son.

Militant in his approach, his son a carbon copy, the large man stopped in front of William and thrust out his hand. "Pleased to meet you. I'm Jan, Gracie's father."

William's throat dried.

"I want to thank you for getting Gracie back to me."

Despite his words, his expression remained unchanged. Stoic.

After nodding several times, seeing none of his friends would talk for him, William said, "It's fine."

"This is Gracie's brother, Austin."

Unlike his father, Austin didn't offer William or any of the others his hand.

"We owe you a great debt and would like to extend our hospitality to you for as long as you'd like it."

William looked at Austin. Maybe he imagined the slight raising of his lip. The faintest snarl. "Thank you?" He said. More a question than a show of gratitude.

"Dad, Austin." Gracie came into the room, her voice echoing in the otherwise silent hall. Every person in there seemed to hold their breath. "I thought you were going to wait for me?"

The slightest softening of her dad, he said, "We couldn't find you, sweetheart."

Gracie made her way through the tables to the group. "Sorry, I was hoping to introduce you formally. And to tell you to ignore Austin. He always looks miserable."

Clearly her older brother, Austin's expression remained unchanged.

"He's a sweetheart when you get to know him."

Hawk raised an eyebrow. "I'll take your word for that."

Olga snorted a laugh.

"Anyway." Jan clapped his hands, the connection whipping around the room like a thunder crack. "Please treat this place like your own for as long as you see fit. I'll look forward to getting to know you all better."

As Gracie's brother and dad left the hall, Gracie sat down at the table.

"I know he just welcomed us," Artan said, "but nothing else about your dad or brother looked pleased to see us here."

Gracie batted the air with her hand. "He lightens up when you get to know him better."

"And Austin?" Olga said.

"He doesn't. He's always serious. Always angry."

Olga raised an eyebrow. "Sounds like a sweetheart."

"He's loyal," Gracie said. "He'll have your back whenever you need it."

"Our back, or *your* back?" Olga said.

William cut in. "Should we be moving on, Gracie?"

She shook her head. "No. Not at all. Dad meant what he said. You're welcome here and you're our guests. Please stay as long as you'd like. We want you here."

"But we're closer to the wall. We've had a rest. I think we should move on." Even as William said it, the aches in his body throbbed as if in protest.

"Look, just stay a while," Gracie said. "Until you're properly rested at least. Dad has an enormous responsibility in this place. The lives of over two hundred people rely on him. He takes that seriously. We have food here. Shelter. Warmth. At least get fully fit and rested. Also, I can take you to the wall. Show you what it's all about."

William gulped. "We're that close?"

Gracie smiled. "We are."

William looked at the others around the table. Dianna nodded straight away. Artan next. Hawk shrugged, and Matilda nodded. Max said, "I could do with a few days off."

"Olga?" William said.

"I reckon we should stay."

Gracie clapped her hands and bounced where she sat. "Amazing. Now come with me. I have something to show you."

∼

MANY OF THE corridors looked the same, but with a bit of time, William would probably learn his way around the place. Where most entrances to the rooms were single doors, Gracie stopped in front of a set of double doors. A wide grin, she said, "We call this room the pleasure dome." She pressed the button, and the doors opened, a bright blue glow spilling from the room.

William gasped when he walked in. A domed ceiling at least twenty feet tall at its highest spot. Covered in moving pictures, there were trees around them and clouds above in an azure sky. "What is this?"

"They're screens," Gracie said.

A yellow, red, and green bird with a long thick beak flew overhead. It landed on the branch of a vibrant tree. Moisture hung in the warm air.

"We spend a lot of time underground," Gracie said. "This room is where we come to lift our spirits. It has different settings. This is a rain forest."

"And it's real?" Max said.

"It was once. You're watching recorded footage."

"So someone has been here?"

"Yeah, when it existed," Gracie said.

Max's shoulders slumped. "It doesn't exist anymore?"

"Who knows?" Gracie shrugged. "This place is on the other side of the planet."

Matilda turned on the spot, her jaw hanging loose. "It's beautiful." She reached out and held William's hand. The door closed, the back of it a screen that slotted into the others. It fully immersed them in the experience. Matilda pressed a soft kiss against William's right cheek. Her warm breath tickled the back of his neck when she whispered in his ear, "I think we've made the right choice. I think we can call this place home for now. I love you."

No wonder they called it the pleasure dome. Every one of their group smiled. Max and Olga held hands. Hawk's stoicism had softened, and he'd moved closer to Dianna. Artan grinned. Maybe they could stay here for a while. William kissed Matilda again. "I love you too."

MICHAEL ROBERTSON

. . .

END OF BOOK EIGHT.

Thank you for reading *Between Fury and Fear*: Book Eight of Beyond These Walls.

Have you checked out *Fury:* Book one in Tales from beyond These Walls? It's a standalone story set in the city of Fury, and is set at the same time as this book. I debated calling it book nine in the series because now is the best time to read it, but I decided against it because it doesn't continue the story for the main characters.

If you're yet to read it, go to www.michaelrobertson.co.uk to check out *Fury:* Book one in Tales from Beyond These Walls.

Before the Dawn: Book Nine of Beyond These Walls is now available for pre-order. While it's on pre-order, you can make a saving and get it for £1.99 / £2.99 rather than £2.99 / $3.99. You can get the book at www.michaelrobertson.co.uk

Support The Author

Dear reader, as an independent author I don't have the resources of a huge publisher. If you like my work and would like to see more from me in the future, there are two things you can do to help: leaving a review, and a word-of-mouth referral.

Releasing a book takes many hours and hundreds of dollars.

I love to write, and would love to continue to do so. All I ask is that you leave an Amazon review. It shows other readers that you've enjoyed the book and will encourage them to give it a try too. The review can be just one sentence, or as long as you like.

FURY: BOOK ONE OF TALES FROM BEYOND THESE WALLS - CHAPTER ONE

"I'm trying to treat today like any other, Mum," Reuben said. "I'm *really* trying." He laid the bread flat and buttered it. When he'd finished, he layered on the thin slices of cheese. "I'm going for a run to see Malcolm. Then I need to get a few things from the shop." Butterflies danced in his stomach, flitting between anxiety and excitement. He took a steadying breath. "Yep, it's just like any other day." But it wasn't just like any other day. He didn't need his mum to tell him that.

Reuben shook with adrenaline. He tried to fill Malcolm's bottle with water and ended up with as much on his hands as in the bottle. "Eighteen today!" He screwed on the lid. "It always seemed so far away. I've been training hard like you said. Working at this my whole life. Dad will be so proud. That is, if they think I'm ready. I am ready, aren't I?"

Very little room to move in his bedsit, breadcrumbs covered the end of Reuben's bed from where he'd made the sandwich. He swiped them away, grabbed his shoes, and sat on the end. His mattress' old springs creaked. He tied the laces tight. "Yep, I'll just keep training. It's like any other day.

I'll go out for a run and keep busy. I'm gaining nothing waiting here."

While packing his backpack, the cheese sandwich wrapped in brown cloth, he repeated, "I'll see Malcolm on my run and then go to the shop to get a few bits. It's just like any other day."

Reuben opened his front door, letting in the fresh spring morning. The sun shone on the city. The slightest chill gave the wind teeth. He called over his shoulder as he stepped outside, "Bye, Mum. See you later." Slamming the door behind him, he took off at a jog down the main road.

By foot or on a bicycle were the best ways to travel around Fury. The city was too small for any larger modes of transport, and the streets were too tight to accommodate them. Not that they had any other vehicles. Other than their dogs, they had no tech in Fury. None of the neighbouring communities were willing to trade anything else.

The river Rend ran through the city. A two-hundred-foot bridge stretched across it. Malcolm lived beneath the bridge. He'd always said he liked it there. That he liked the cold winters and damp springs. No point in challenging the lie. What could Reuben do? Offer to let him stay in his tiny house? And what would his mum think? She called his greatest strength his biggest weakness. He was too soft. He gave people too much.

∼

Despite the enormous steel wall surrounding the city, the wind always blew hard along the river, entering through the grates beneath their fortified boundary. It dropped the temperature by a few degrees.

Out of breath from the run, Reuben picked his way down the steep riverbank with cautious steps. He unslung his backpack and removed the sandwich and drink. Malcolm always slept beneath a red blanket and always refused the offer of anything warmer. He took his daily sandwich and water, but insisted he needed nothing else.

"If sir would like to look at the menu," Reuben said to the red blanket, "I think he might be pleasantly surprised. Today, for the one thousandth, three hundredth, and eighty-seventh day in a row, I present sir with"—he held the wrapped sandwich out on the palm of his hand—"a cheese sandwich and Fury's finest bottled water."

Reuben's chest tightened when his friend didn't move. "Malcolm?"

Reuben pulled the blanket away to reveal a log.

A deep and booming laugh, it resonated in the tight space beneath the bridge as Malcolm appeared from the other side. His hair a six-inch halo of white, he had a wide grin filled with wonky teeth. Mirth shone in his brilliant blue eyes. The man walked with a stoop from so many years of sleeping rough. It masked his six-foot-plus stature. He pointed at Reuben and laughed again. "Got ya!"

While holding his hammering heart, Reuben rolled his eyes.

"I don't know whether to laugh about catching you out," Malcom said, "or to cry because no matter how many times I pull this trick, you fall for it. Do you really think you're going to find me dead beneath this bridge *every* morning?"

His face hot with his shame, Reuben shrugged. "You've told me not to worry about you, but that doesn't mean I don't. Is that such a crime?" He threw the cheese sandwich at his friend. After Malcolm caught it, he threw the bottle of water.

"Come here!" Malcolm hugged Reuben before stepping back and holding him by the tops of his shoulders. "Thank you. As always."

Reuben shrugged, avoiding eye contact, his face on fire.

"Wait a minute." Malcom gripped tighter, and Reuben did his best to hide his wince. An old man, older than his years because of his lifestyle, but he still had the strength to crush rocks in his gnarled hands. "Today's the day, right?"

It pulled Reuben's attention back to his friend. "I hope so."

"Nothing's arrived yet?"

"It's early. There's a lot of the day still ahead of us." Always looking out for other people. His greatest weakness. Trying to make Malcolm feel better about his disappointment.

"That there is. So how do you plan to spend your last day of freedom?"

"Boredom more like. And we don't know if it *is* the last day."

"Someone's fucked up big time if it isn't." Malcom sat down on the riverbank, his long legs folding into triangles, his knobbly knees pointing at the underside of the bridge.

Reuben sat next to him. "Are you sure there's nothing more I can do for you? Nothing else you need?"

Malcolm's right cheek bulged with his food. He spoke through a clamped jaw, his beard covered in breadcrumbs. "You do enough."

"I don't think I do."

"You do more than anyone else."

"That's hardly a yardstick."

"Honestly." Malcolm took another large bite, which he didn't stow in his cheek this time. His voice muffled, he said, "I appreciate everything you do for me. I don't need or want anything else."

The wind hummed beneath the wide bridge. The river churned with its fast current. It filled the silence. Gave them permission to just be.

After a few minutes, Reuben said, "Do you really think it will come today?"

"They'd be mad to not want you," Malcolm said.

And what did Reuben expect? Malcom didn't have the answers. He'd say what Reuben needed to hear.

~

THE BELL over the shop door tinkled. Reuben had spent the past few hours with Malcolm. Better he killed time with his friend than waiting at home bothering his mum. After he'd filled his basket, Patricia took his items and placed them into his bag. Bread, cheese … "You still feeding Malcolm?"

"If I don't …" But Reuben left the thought hanging. "Yes."

Careful not to crush them, Patricia placed the bunch of tulips in last, leaving them poking from the top of his bag. "For your mum?"

Reuben shrugged.

"You're a good boy." She smiled, dimples in her round cheeks. Because she ran the shop, she got more food than most.

He lifted his chest. "Eighteen today."

"Oh, shit!" Patricia clapped a hand to her mouth. Her green eyes widened, her hand muffling her words. "I'm sorry. I don't usually swear. But … oh my! Today's the day, right?"

Reuben shifted his stance. He shrugged. "I hope so." What would he tell all these people if it didn't happen? How could he come back here tomorrow and make her feel better about his disappointment?

"Waste of time if you ask me." Ken, although ever present in the shop, rarely spoke. He sat in a chair in the corner, wearing the frown of someone deep in thought, but with nothing in front of him to warrant his posturing, and very little spewing from his mouth to justify it.

"No one asked you, Ken," Patricia shot back at him.

"Well, they should. I think people are afraid because I tell it how it is."

"You tell it how you see it," Patricia said. She rolled her eyes at Reuben. "There's a big difference."

"To you maybe!"

"Anyway, there's enough misery in this world without you adding to it." Patricia winked. "I swear, if they made murder legal in this city, I'd seriously consider it."

"Not if I got you first," Ken said.

Patricia moved across in front of him, blocking him from Reuben's line of sight. "Don't listen to him. You get home now. I bet you it's already arrived."

～

Just past noon by the time Reuben got home. A warm spring day, his clothes clung to his sweating skin. He paused before going in. No sign of the delivery. His shoulders slumped. His heart heavy. It wouldn't do any good to wait outside all day. Better to face it.

Reuben unlocked his door, the hinges creaking as he entered. "Don't suppose the delivery person has been yet, Mum?" Although why he wasted his time asking ... If there had been a delivery, it would have been waiting for him. "Do you think they've forgotten about me? Or have they rejected me? I didn't even consider that." He'd considered it. He'd considered it every damn day for the past few years, but his mum didn't need to hear his self-doubt.

His mum's favourite vase, a clay pot Reuben had made for her at school years ago. He filled it with water and arranged the white tulips. The lump in his throat tightened his words. "Maybe it's a good thing. It will be nice to thank the person for delivering it when they turn up."

∽

Reuben had spent the afternoon watching the door like a dog waiting for their owner to come home. By the time he sat down for dinner, it had gotten dark outside. No one went out after dark in Fury. Scrambled eggs and toast, he pushed it around his plate, the knot in his stomach banishing his hunger. He tried a mouthful of the rubbery egg, the salty butter, the crunchy toast. His favourite meal, but it tasted like shit today.

He shoved the plate away and blinked at the window by the door. His eyes were sore from trying to see through the darkness. "They're not coming, are they, Mum?"

The tulips remained in the vase on the kitchen worktop. He moved them so his mum could see them better. While arranging the flowers, he said, "I've done everything required of me. I'm fit. I'm healthy. I'm keen …"

His mother's eyes sparkled. He'd drawn a thousand sketches of her over the years. His current favourite sat in the frame he'd made. Never a perfect drawing, but what would be? Perfect would be her still here now. He'd arranged trinkets and ornaments in front of the picture. A small stone heart. He'd spent the night of her funeral whittling it despite being blinded by his tears. It sat next to a wooden stick wrapped in red, blue, and yellow fabric. Acorns and fir cones, the acorns wrinkled. They'd been there since autumn. She'd died seven years previously. It still stung like it had happened yesterday. Neighbours and friends had plied him with all the usual clichés like *time's a great healer,* and *it'll get easier.* If that was the case, seven years was nowhere near long enough.

The eyes he'd drawn had taken on a life of their own. Right now they said what he didn't want to hear. But he had to accept it. "You're right." Reuben bit his quivering bottom lip. His view blurred. His voice wavered. "I'm not getting a delivery today. And it's not like they'll ever tell me why. Nothing. Ghosted. Application rejected. Now get on with your sad and lonely life. Dig holes somewhere. Work in manufacturing or agriculture." He sighed. "I wanted to make you and Dad proud of me."

Reuben drew a deep and stuttered breath. He nodded at the picture. "Tomorrow's another day. I know. Maybe tomorrow, eh?" The flame of hope in his chest flickered only to be smothered again when the shadows closed in. They'd not chosen him. To deny the reality would only prolong his suffering. No matter what tomorrow brought, his next step had to be acceptance.

Falling onto his creaking bed, Reuben rolled over onto his side, pulled his knees up to his chest, and curled into the foetal position. Tomorrow might be another day, but it wouldn't be like any other. Tomorrow, like when his mum had passed, would mark a fundamental change. The day he had to accept the life he'd spent the past several years planning, didn't belong to him. A dream that would never become reality.

Thank you for reading chapter one of *Fury: Tales from Beyond These Walls book one.* You can check out the entire book at www.michaelrobertson.co.uk

BOOK ONE OF TALES FROM BEYOND THESE WALLS
A POST-APOCALYPTIC SURVIVAL THRILLER
FURY
MICHAEL ROBERTSON

ABOUT THE AUTHOR

Like most children born in the seventies, Michael grew up with Star Wars in his life, along with other great stories like Labyrinth, The Neverending Story, and as he grew older, the Alien franchise. An obsessive watcher of movies and consumer of stories, he found his mind wandering to stories of his own.

Those stories had to come out.

He hopes you enjoy reading his work as much as he does creating it.

Contact
www.michaelrobertson.co.uk
subscribers@michaelrobertson.co.uk

READER GROUP

Join my reader group for all my latest releases and special offers. You'll also receive these four FREE books. You can unsubscribe at any time.

Go to www.michaelrobertson.co.uk

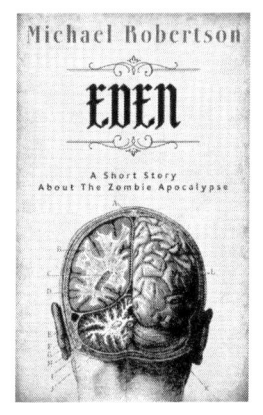

MICHAEL ROBERTSON

ALSO BY MICHAEL ROBERTSON

THE SHADOW ORDER:

The Shadow Order

The First Mission - Book Two of The Shadow Order

The Crimson War - Book Three of The Shadow Order

Eradication - Book Four of The Shadow Order

Fugitive - Book Five of The Shadow Order

Enigma - Book Six of The Shadow Order

Prophecy - Book Seven of The Shadow Order

The Faradis - Book Eight of The Shadow Order

The Complete Shadow Order Box Set - Books 1 - 8

∽

NEON HORIZON:

The Blind Spot - A Science Fiction Thriller - Neon Horizon Book One.

Prime City - A Science Fiction Thriller - Neon Horizon Book Two.

Bounty Hunter - A Science Fiction Thriller - Neon Horizon Book Three.

Neon Horizon - Books 1 - 3 Box Set - A Science Fiction Thriller.

∽

THE ALPHA PLAGUE:

The Alpha Plague: A Post-Apocalyptic Action Thriller

The Alpha Plague 2

The Alpha Plague 3

The Alpha Plague 4

The Alpha Plague 5

The Alpha Plague 6

The Alpha Plague 7

The Alpha Plague 8

The Complete Alpha Plague Box Set - Books 1 - 8

∿

BEYOND THESE WALLS:

Protectors - Book one of Beyond These Walls

National Service - Book two of Beyond These Walls

Retribution - Book three of Beyond These Walls

Collapse - Book four of Beyond These Walls

After Edin - Book five of Beyond These Walls

Three Days - Book six of Beyond These Walls

The Asylum - Book seven of Beyond These Walls

Between Fury and Fear - Book eight of Beyond These Walls

Before the Dawn - Book nine of Beyond These Walls

Beyond These Walls - Books 1 - 6 Box Set

∿

TALES FROM BEYOND THESE WALLS:

Fury - Book one of Tales From Beyond These Walls

∿

OFF-KILTER TALES:

The Girl in the Woods - A Ghost's Story - Off-Kilter Tales Book One

Rat Run - A Post-Apocalyptic Tale - Off-Kilter Tales Book Two

∼

Masked - A Psychological Horror

∼

CRASH:
Crash - A Dark Post-Apocalyptic Tale
Crash II: Highrise Hell
Crash III: There's No Place Like Home
Crash IV: Run Free
Crash V: The Final Showdown

∼

NEW REALITY:
New Reality: Truth
New Reality 2: Justice
New Reality 3: Fear

∼

Audiobooks:

The Alpha Plague Audiobooks:
US - Audiobook for The Alpha Plague Books 1 - 3.
UK - Audiobook for The Alpha Plague Books 1 - 3.
Germany - Audiobook for The Alpha Plague Books 1 - 3.
France - Audiobook for The Alpha Plague Books 1 - 3.

US - Audiobook for The Alpha Plague Book 4.
UK - Audiobook for The Alpha Plague Book 4.
Germany - Audiobook for The Alpha Plague Book 4.
France - Audiobook for The Alpha Plague Book 4.

US - Audiobook for The Alpha Plague Book 5.
UK - Audiobook for The Alpha Plague Book 5.
Germany - Audiobook for The Alpha Plague Book 5.
France - Audiobook for The Alpha Plague Book 5.

US - Audiobook for The Alpha Plague Book 6.
UK - Audiobook for The Alpha Plague Book 6.
Germany - Audiobook for The Alpha Plague Book 6.
France - Audiobook for The Alpha Plague Book 6.

US - Audiobook for The Alpha Plague books 7 & 8 box set.
UK - Audiobook for The Alpha Plague books 7 & 8 box set.
Germany - Audiobook for The Alpha Plague books 7 & 8 box set.
France - Audiobook for The Alpha Plague books 7 & 8 box set.

Beyond These Walls Audiobooks

US - Audiobook for Beyond These Walls Books 1 - 3.
UK - Audiobook for Beyond These Walls Books 1 - 3.
Germany - Audiobook for Beyond These Walls Books 1 - 3.
France - Audiobook for Beyond These Walls Books 1 - 3.

US - Audiobook for Beyond These Walls Books 4 - 6.
UK - Audiobook for Beyond These Walls Books 4 - 6.
Germany - Audiobook for Beyond These Walls Books 4 - 6.
France - Audiobook for Beyond These Walls Books 4 - 6.

The Shadow Order Audiobooks

US - Audiobook for The Shadow Order Books 1 - 3.

UK - Audiobook for The Shadow Order Books 1 - 3.

Germany - Audiobook for The Shadow Order Books 1 - 3.

France - Audiobook for The Shadow Order Books 1 - 3.

The Shadow Order books 4 - 6 coming to audio soon.

Rat Run Audiobook:

US - Audiobook for Rat Run.

UK - Audiobook for Rat Run.

Germany - Audiobook for Rat Run.

France - Audiobook for Rat Run.

Crash Audiobooks

US - Audiobook for Crash.

UK - Audiobook for Crash.

Germany - Audiobook for Crash.

France - Audiobook for Crash.

US - Audiobook for Crash II.

UK - Audiobook for Crash II.

Germany - Audiobook for Crash II.

France - Audiobook for Crash II.

US - Audiobook for Crash III.

UK - Audiobook for Crash III.

Germany - Audiobook for Crash III.

France - Audiobook for Crash III.

US - Audiobook for Crash IV.

UK - Audiobook for Crash IV.
Germany - Audiobook for Crash IV.
France - Audiobook for Crash IV.

Crash V coming to audiobook soon.

Printed in Great Britain
by Amazon